BE CAREFUL
WHAT YOU WISH FOR

TEEN Witch

#2

BE CAREFUL
WHAT YOU WISH FOR

MEGAN BARNES

SCHOLASTIC INC.
New York Toronto London Auckland Sydney

ISBN 0-590-41297-3

12 11 10 9 8 7 6 5 4 3 2 1   8 9/8 0 1 2 3/9

Printed in the U.S.A.   01

First Scholastic printing, December 1988

Chapter 1

Sarah Connell was the only person in the Waterview High School cafeteria who knew the real reason why the day's special, Tasty Meat Loaf, had mysteriously vanished. She was standing patiently in line with her friends, when Tina Jordan gave an anguished yelp.

"Hey, guys," Tina said, peering at the black menu board with its white stick-on letters, "prepare to die. Today's the day for mystery meat loaf." Tina rolled her eyes expressively and gave a resigned sigh. A stunning black girl with a perfect figure, she patted her flat stomach as if checking for hidden cellulite. "Oh, well, I need to lose a few pounds, and this is a great place to start."

"Tasty Meat Loaf," Micki Davis groaned. "Who are they trying to kid, anyway?" She started to reach for a knife and fork when Sarah, her best friend, who was standing behind her, nudged her gently.

"It's okay, Micki," Sarah whispered urgently. "They're going to change it any minute to that vegetarian alphabet soup you like. So get a spoon and some crackers." She leaned close to her friend, talking between closed lips like a ventriloquist.

"Yeah?" Micki's brown eyes widened in surprise. She had learned a few weeks ago to trust Sarah's judgment in these things, so she quickly moved her tray forward.

Within minutes, Sarah's prediction came true. Ms. Colson, the cafeteria supervisor, hurried over to the menu board, clutching a handful of letters.

"I'd like to buy a vowel," Matt Neville yelled, getting a big laugh from the kids in line. Ms. Colson turned to glare at him, and Matt threw both hands up apologetically. "I'm just kidding, Ms. Colson," he said politely. "What's the new special going to be?"

"Tasty Meat Loaf II," Kirk Tanner whispered to Micki, who chuckled appreciatively.

"You'll see soon enough," Ms. Colson said sharply. She began changing the board, peeling off the old letters and placing a capital "V" in the upper right-hand corner.

"V! Ohmigosh," Heather Larson said. "They played a rerun of that on TV last night. It was really gross," she added, her blonde curls swinging as she talked. "Do you remember the scene where the lizard. . . ."

Sarah didn't listen to the rest of Heather's comments because Micki had edged a little closer to her and mouthed a silent thanks. "Did you do something to the meat loaf?" she asked in a low voice.

"I'm afraid I can't take credit for it," Sarah said, her brown eyes full of laughter.

"You mean it disappeared all by itself?"

Sarah put a solemn expression on her face, but Micki, who had known her for years, could see that she was just seconds away from giggling. "Not quite," she said slowly. "But Ms. Colson did — accidentally." She paused for effect, and Micki punched her playfully on the arm. "There was a box of sugar and a box of salt sitting side by side on the counter," she whispered, "and she got them mixed up."

"No!"

Sarah nodded. "Yes! And I didn't have a thing to do with it. Not that I'm disappointed," she added firmly. "Ms. Colson's Tasty Meat Loaf is enough to turn anyone into — "

"A vegetarian," Matt said, joining the conversation. Matt, a sandy-haired boy with glasses, was one of the brightest kids in the class and had been friends with Sarah and Micki since kindergarten. He was wearing his favorite outfit today, a pair of neatly pressed khakis with a pastel shirt, and his narrow face was creased in a smile. "That's amazing," he said, watching as Ms. Colson finished spelling out the new special. "I wonder what happened to the old special?" he said to no one in particular. "I thought it was indestructible — you know, 'The Meat Loaf That Wouldn't Die.' "

Heather Larson turned to smile at him, and he looked pleased, even though Sarah knew Heather wasn't his type.

The line started creeping forward once more, and Sarah caught herself staring at the menu board. It read: VEGETARIAN ALPHABET SOUP, just like she had known it would. The letters were slanting downward, and the stem was missing off the letter P. She had known about that, too. She ran her fingers through her tangle of chestnut curls and smiled. She was getting better at this — she really was.

The vegetable soup was only a small demonstration of her talents; she could do many other things that no one knew about. No one but Micki, of course. And Micki would never tell. First of all, because she was her best friend, and secondly, because she could keep a secret better than anyone in the world.

Sarah looked at Heather, deep in conversation with Matt, and thought how surprised they would be if they ever guessed the range of her powers. They'd be stunned! After all, she was the only person in the cafeteria who could make objects appear and disappear, who could mix up magic potions, who could travel through time and space. And that was just the beginning. She could cast spells, uncast them if she followed the directions carefully, and make perfect strangers fall in love with her. She could even make herself invisible, at least for short periods of time.

No one else in the cafeteria had the slightest inkling of the amazing things Sarah could do. But how could they? she thought, looking fondly at her friends. No one else in the cafeteria was a teen witch!

Finally, Sarah and her friends got their lunches and sat down. Matt pulled out some history notes to study, and Sarah and Micki listened as Heather described the new boy she had met at the Pizza Palace.

"You met him?" Micki asked. "I thought you said earlier you didn't even know his name." A friendly girl with short red hair and a creamy complexion, Micki was far more thoughtful and observant than her friend Sarah. In many ways, the two girls were exact opposites — Sarah tended to speak without thinking and do things on impulse, while Micki weighed every decision carefully. Even their taste in clothes was different. Today Sarah was decked out in a safari jacket with a wild animal print blouse, and Micki was dressed more conservatively in a simple pleated skirt and navy-blue sweater.

"I didn't exactly *meet* him," Heather admitted in her little-girl voice. "He took my order." She paused and cupped her chin in her hand. "An individual pepperoni pizza and a small Coke."

Tina Jordan almost choked on her soup. "How romantic!" she said wryly. "And what did he say?"

"He said. . . ." Heather had to stop and think a minute. "He said 'Coming right up.' " Her heart-shaped face brightened with pleasure. "But it was the *way* he said it."

"Heather," Micki pleaded, "don't go getting a crazy crush on him. He probably says that to everyone."

"Maybe he does," Heather said staunchly, spooning up her soup. She took small, delicate sips that reminded Sarah of a cat. "But he *meant* it with me. I know he did."

Micki and Sarah exchanged a look. Heather was one of the sweetest girls they knew, even if she wasn't one of the brightest.

"I'm sure he did," Sarah said kindly.

Later that day, when Sarah and Micki were having an after-school snack in Sarah's kitchen, the conversation turned to Heather.

"Hey, I've got an idea," Micki said, cutting into a huge slab of devil's food cake. "Why don't you snap your fingers and make this new boy fall in love with Heather? She'd be thrilled." Micki was only half-kidding, her brown eyes teasing.

"I tried that once before, remember?" Sarah said, reaching for the milk. "Cody Rice." She made a face, remembering the love spell she had cast on a handsome new boy at Waterview. It had been such a total disaster, that she had to ask her Aunt Pam — who was also a witch — to step in and help. "Anyway, I don't snap my fingers to cast a spell. They only do that on TV. I can make things happen just by concentrating on them."

"Really?" Micki was impressed. She still couldn't get over the fact that Sarah — her best friend since kindergarten — was a witch. Sarah had seemed like an ordinary girl until her thirteenth birthday a few months before, when her Aunt Pam had explained about these new, incredible powers. It had taken a little while for Sarah to get used to the idea.

Some of her first attempts with her new powers were pretty funny, Micki remembered, because Sarah was only a beginner. An apprentice witch, her Aunt Pam called it. The way Sarah explained it to Micki, the magic was something you really had to work at, and of course, you had to use it responsibly. Aunt Pam was the only person in the family who knew that Sarah was a witch, and Micki was glad that she spent a lot of time with her, talking and asking questions.

"Who do *you* think is cute this year?" Sarah asked, cutting into her thoughts. Micki was surprised at the question. Outside of Sarah's brief experience with Cody Rice, the whole world of dating was a mystery to them.

"Gee, I don't know. I haven't given it much thought." Micki set her cup down carefully on the placemat so it wouldn't leave a ring on the polished oak table. Usually the Connell house was bursting with noise and laughter, but today both Simon and Nicole, Sarah's older brother and sister, were out, and the kitchen was quiet. "What brought that on?" she asked laughing.

"Oh, I don't know," Sarah said, inspecting one of her short fingernails. She had always thought that long nails were a waste of time, but after seeing some of the new nail designs in the magazines, she had decided to let hers grow. Sarah's dream was to be a fashion designer, so she always liked to keep up on new things, even when they were crazy fads, like gluing rhinestones to your fingertips. "I guess I was thinking about Heather, and I was sort of fantasizing that if you could date any boy in the world, who would it be?"

"Any boy in the world?" Micki's face lit up. "Wow — that would be a trip. I think I'd start with Rob Lowe, and then work my way through Kirk Cameron, Michael J. Fox, and River Phoenix."

"I meant any boy in our *school*," Sarah amended.

"That's not what you said," Micki told her reproachfully.

"Maybe not, but even witches have their limitations."

"Oh, I see," Micki said, going along with the joke. "You mean that you *would* get me any boy in the world, if you could — "

"But I can't so I won't," Sarah said with a chuckle.

They rinsed off their cups and saucers and then, Sarah was struck by a wild idea. What if she really *could* get Micki any boy she wanted? Any boy at Waterview, that is. Wouldn't Micki be thrilled? And she'd never guess that Sarah had anything to do with it — not after this little conversation today. Sarah had practically told her that she was off love spells forever.

All she had to do now was figure out which one Micki liked.

Chapter 2

Sarah had always found that if she thought about a problem before she went to sleep, the answer usually came to her in the morning. So she wasn't surprised when a terrific idea about Micki struck her at breakfast the very next day.

Breakfast at the Connells' was a pretty hectic affair. Since Sarah's father, David Connell, was a busy pediatrician, it was often the only time the whole family sat down together. And since Dr. Connell kept a suite of offices in a separate wing of the house, breakfast was usually punctuated by the sound of crying babies and a steady *beeeepp* as his nurse buzzed him on the intercom.

That morning was no exception. Dr. Connell had been called to the phone three times, and the last time, he motioned for Sarah to take over the cooking. "Stir it gently, and don't bruise the eggs," he said, pointing to a gloppy yellow mass in the iron skillet.

"What is it?" Sarah asked, dismayed. Her father's cooking experiments usually turned out to be disasters. He was particularly interested in health food, and most of his recipes included wheat germ, kelp, or both.

"It's eggs Florentine," he said, looking surprised. "They served it to the crowned heads of Europe," he added, reaching for the phone.

"No wonder they lost their heads," Simon Connell muttered. Simon, Sarah's seventeen-year-old brother, peered into the skillet, and pretended to clutch his throat in agony. He staggered backward dramatically, nearly bumping into his mother, who was stuffing papers in her briefcase.

"Simon, please," she said automatically. Karen Connell was a tall, attractive woman with glossy black hair and dark eyes. Her work as a guidance counselor at a small private school was demanding, but she loved her job. "Just sit down and eat."

"Why don't you have some, Mom?" Simon

said mischievously. "Here, I'll clear a place for you."

"That's okay," Mrs. Connell said quickly. "I have an early morning meeting with the principal, so I better run." She threw her coat over her arm and dashed out the door before he could say another word.

As Sarah stirred, snatches of her father's and Simon's conversation drifted across her mind. "How are they ranked?" her father was saying, talking about some team. There was a pause, and then she heard Simon say, "I think they were ranked fifth. . . ."

Ranked. That was it! she thought excitedly. She could get Micki to rank all the boys in school, just like they ranked teams. That way, she could find out who Micki really liked, and she could put her plan into action. Micki might think the question was a little odd, but Sarah would make it sound scientific. She could even pretend it was part of a school project.

She could hardly wait to see Micki at lunch and get to work. She slid back her chair just as her sister Nicole drifted into the kitchen. Nicole, at fifteen, was a preppy vision — shiny blonde hair swept off her face with barrettes, a gray sweater, watchplaid wool skirt and charcoal-gray knee socks. She started to sit down at the oak breakfast table and realized her mistake too late.

"Glad you could join us," Dr. Connell said heartily. "We're enjoying a breakfast fit for a king," he added, winking at Sarah and Simon.

When Sarah left the house, the bright sunlight hit her the moment she stepped outside. It was going to be another dazzling southern California day, and the warm air lifted Sarah's spirits. The perfect day to start Project Micki!

Sarah fidgeted all through lunch, and finally saw an opening when Heather Larson decided to tell the plot of a movie she had seen on TV that weekend. Heather's plot descriptions were always colorful — if completely inaccurate — and she often jumbled up two or three movies together. Sarah waited until everyone was enthralled by Heather's recounting of *King Kong Part II*, then nudged Micki under the table.

"Uh, Micki," she said in a low voice. "I need your help with something." She whipped out her notebook and began flipping through the pages as if she were looking for a homework assignment.

"Sure, what is it?" Micki pushed aside the

remains of her apple pie and brushed a lock of auburn hair off her forehead. "Not differential equations, is it?"

"Uh, no, not quite." Sarah tapped her pencil thoughtfully against the notebook, wondering where to begin. She pretended to be reading from her notes. "Okay, here goes. Question number one: If I asked you to pick the five cutest boys in the lunchroom, who would they be?"

"What?" Micki gave her a look that said she was clearly insane, and Sarah's hopes plummeted. This was going to be trickier than she had thought. She obviously needed a better approach if she wanted Micki to take this seriously.

"This is on the level. It's for an assignment," she said, putting on her most reassuring voice. "Sort of a research project."

"A research project — for what class?" Micki sounded suspicious.

Sarah was ready this time. "For Mrs. Hendricks's Social Problems," she said innocently. She had picked one of the classes they didn't have together.

"Sounds funny to me," Micki said, still not convinced.

"Please," Sarah said, "just answer the question." She glanced at the clock. The fourth period bell would ring any moment, and she hadn't gotten anywhere.

"It's a pretty weird question, even for Mrs. Hendricks to dream up." Micki could be surprisingly stubborn, and Sarah decided she'd better improvise quickly if she wanted Micki to cooperate.

"Well, we're studying people in groups and how they, uh, interact," Sarah said, making it up as she went along.

Micki shrugged. "Well, it seems a little silly, but if it's that important to you. . . ." She glanced around the crowded lunchroom. "Let's see, Jonathan Brooks is cute. . . ."

"Jonathan Brooks! He's such a preppy," Sarah blurted out. Micki looked annoyed so Sarah said, "Okay, Jonathan Brooks is number one." She tapped the pencil impatiently. "Now I need four more."

"Oh, gee, I don't know," Micki said vaguely. "I hate doing this. It seems awful to put a number on people, like they were a grade of hamburger."

"The names." Sarah thrust her chin forward and waited.

The bell rang then, and Micki reached for

her purse, but Sarah clamped her hand over it with a viselike grip. "Four more."

Micki's eyes flickered around the cafeteria, and she said quickly, "Uh, Jeff Tyson, Scott Randall, Rafe Carter, and Tim Cassidy."

Sarah smiled and relaxed her grip. "Very good, Micki. I knew you could do it," she said sweetly.

"Wow, I'm glad that's over," Micki muttered.

Micki gave her strange looks all through French class that afternoon, but Sarah ignored them and concentrated on the text that Mme. Devereau was reading. Mme. Devereau was very fond of reading aloud to them from the great French poets and novelists. They were supposed to write down everything they heard and turn in their dictations at the end of class. Since Sarah only understood about one word in five, she had no idea whether her teacher was reading from a novel, a poem, or a grocery list. She scribbled down what she could and waited for the class discussion that always followed.

Usually Sarah found Madame's lectures incredibly dull, but today was an exception. The topic was romantic heroes, and Madame began the discussion by asking who would like to describe the perfect hero. Heather raised her hand.

"Tom Cruise," she said promptly. Everyone cracked up, and Heather looked puzzled.

Mme. Devereau's lips twitched as she gently said, "I didn't mean American movie stars, Heather. I meant romantic heroes in medieval legends. The ones that we've talked about in class."

"You know, Heather, all those guys who wore suits of armor and rode around on unicorns," Allison Rogers said nastily. Allison was a thin girl with long brown hair who loved putting people down.

"Oh," Heather said, embarrassed. "Well, let me see. I guess the perfect hero was someone who would do anything for his lady love. Even ride his horse off a cliff, if necessary," she added dramatically. "Although it certainly wasn't much fun for the horse." Someone sitting by the window snickered, and she turned to glare at them.

"That's an interesting way of putting it." Mme. Devereau was diplomatic. "Anyone else have any ideas?"

"They put love above everything else in their lives," Kirk Tanner volunteered. Kirk was a tall, good-looking boy with cool gray eyes and a terrific smile. Sarah had had a crush on him for as long as she could remember, and once or twice, she thought that maybe he felt the same way about her. For some reason, though, the timing was never quite right, and the last she'd heard, he was dating a cute cheerleader named Beverly Dobson.

"Go on," Mme. Devereau encouraged.

"Well, they fought battles over love, and they used to storm castles to rescue damsels in distress. . . ."

"Help!" a girl in the back row yelled, but Madame silenced her with a look.

"And they'd even die for love, if they had to."

"That's what I said," Heather muttered, annoyed.

Mme. Devereau apparently thought it was time to steer the discussion around because she said, "Would anyone like to tell me how they would fare in the world today? Would we still admire them?"

Everyone was quiet and then Micki raised her hand.

"They'd be lost in the twentieth century," she insisted. "Totally out of it."

"And why is that?"

"Because we're not looking for guys who can ride unicorns anymore. . . . Sorry, I mean, horses," she said, with a giggle. "And the last thing we need is someone to scale moats or storm castles. The perfect boy today would be" — she paused and looked right at Sarah — "someone who you could really talk to, and who would always be there for you. And it wouldn't matter at all if he was good-looking, or if he was big and strong. He wouldn't even have to look great in a suit of armor!" she finished with a laugh.

Everyone wanted to jump in the discussion then, and Sarah looked at Micki thoughtfully. Did she really mean everything she had just said? Sarah thought over the list of "cute boys" she had picked out of the lunchroom. Jonathan Brooks, Jeff Tyson, Scott Randall . . . something was really wrong here. What in the world was Micki thinking of? she wondered. Those boys didn't fit the description she just gave at all.

She thought about her next step, and decided to check things out with Aunt Pam. Not just because Pamela Huntley was her favorite aunt, and always gave fantastic advice, but because she was also a witch. Sarah glanced at her watch. Almost two o'clock. In just an hour, she could be sitting in Aunt Pam's back room, sipping a cup of tea, telling her all about her wonderful plans for Micki.

Chapter 3

"Perfect timing!" Aunt Pam said happily a little later. She swept Sarah into Plates and Pages, her combination bookstore and tea shop, motioning her to a table that was already set with tea and cakes. "The cinnamon rolls just came out of the oven, and I made them with a lot of gooey caramel, the way you like them."

"How did you know I was coming?" Sarah said, pulling off her red windbreaker and sliding into a chair.

"Oh, we have our ways," Aunt Pam teased. A tall, slender woman with jet-black hair that cascaded over her shoulders, Aunt Pam was one of the most beautiful women Sarah had ever seen. A lot of people thought her taste in clothes was really strange — she called it "early flea market" — but Sarah loved it. She couldn't imagine anyone as dramatic and unusual as Pamela Huntley wearing boring little suits and skirts. Today she looked like she was in a dress rehearsal for *Carmen*. She was wearing a scooped-neck peasant blouse with heavy gold embroidery and a long, wine-colored skirt that flowed around her ankles. She had wrapped a couple of silk scarves around her waist in place of a belt, and half a dozen gold bracelets clanked together on her left wrist.

"So, tell me all the fascinating things that are going on in your life," Aunt Pam said, fixing Sarah with her mysterious golden eyes. She had a way of really listening that was unusual in adults, Sarah thought. Most adults weren't that interested in what kids had to say, but Aunt Pam acted as if you were the only person in the world when she talked with you. She waved her hand at the quiet shop, with its empty aisles. "We won't be disturbed for the rest of the afternoon."

"Are you sure?" Sarah asked surprised. She had often thought that Aunt Pam must be psychic, but her aunt had assured her that she wasn't.

"Of course I'm sure." She pointed to the

CLOSED sign she had mounted in the front bay window. "I always close early on Wednesdays, remember?"

Briefly, Sarah told Aunt Pam about her plan to make a boy fall in love with Micki, and the "cute list" that she had written in the lunchroom. Aunt Pam was silent as Sarah talked, but shook her head slightly from time to time, as if she disapproved of the whole idea. "So the problem, you see, is that Micki picked out these boys who don't seem right for her at all, in fact, they seem totally wrong for her."

Aunt Pam waited a minute before saying anything, idly tracing a design on the paisley tablecloth with the end of her spoon. "You know, this all has a very familiar ring to it," she said finally.

"I know," Sarah said quickly. "You're thinking of that last love spell I did with Cody Rice. I admit, I made a complete mess of things, but this is different — honestly."

"How is it different?" Aunt Pam had a way of getting right to the point.

"Well, for one thing, it's not for me," Sarah said, thinking fast. "I'm not doing it for selfish reasons, I'm doing it to help a friend."

"A friend who may not even want, or need your help," Aunt Pam pointed out. "A friend who would probably be horrified if she knew you were sitting here talking about this."

Sarah thought for a moment. "That may be true," she admitted. "But don't you think you should help people, even if they don't know what's good for them?"

"Ah, but what's good for them?" Aunt Pam fingered a large ring on her left hand. It was a single stone in a delicate gold setting, and Sarah had always admired it. It was impossible to say what color it was, because it changed color so often. Sometimes it was as green as a field of clover, and other times, slate blue, like the ocean on a stormy day. "Should you be the judge of that?"

"Well, I do know her pretty well," Sarah said uncomfortably. Aunt Pam had a way of asking questions Sarah never even thought of, and she was beginning to wish she hadn't told her aunt about Micki.

"I know you do," Aunt Pam said in a soft voice. "And she's very lucky to have a friend like you." She paused. "But my advice, if you really want to help Micki, is to let well enough alone."

"But nothing will happen if I let well enough alone!" Sarah protested. "She'll just go on the way she always does, and no one will ask her out. Because no one seems to see what a terrific person she is. Except for Matt, and he doesn't count, because he's just a friend."

Aunt Pam was firm. "Sarah," she said, laying her hand gently on her niece's arm, "if you want to be a good friend to Micki, let things be. She'll find her own boyfriend, in her own time, in her own way."

It was obvious that Aunt Pam thought she shouldn't use her powers to help Micki, and that she wasn't going to make any helpful suggestions along those lines. So she would just have to do this on her own, Sarah decided. She was positive she could avoid the same mistakes she'd made the last time. She realized now that making a love potion out of a dozen herbs and spices hadn't been the smartest idea in the world, but this time she would use a totally fresh approach. Something without powders or potions, something strictly mental.

When Sarah finally left Aunt Pam's an hour later, the late afternoon sun had vanished, and there was a chill in the air as she hurried up Front Street. A sudden gust of wind propelled her right past the corner of Front and Sixth, where she usually turned, and instead she found herself under the green-and-white-striped awning of Rugby's. Rugby's — the town's most expensive clothing store — was a place that Sarah usually avoided, but today she caught herself staring at a display in the window.

Without really knowing why, she pushed open the heavy glass door, and a salesman appeared as if she had conjured him up. "How may I help you?" He spoke softly, as if they were in a museum.

"Just browsing," Sarah said quickly. What am I doing here? she wondered. She didn't even like the clothes, she thought; they were much too preppy for her taste. She glanced at a display of creamy wool "Genuine Newfoundland Fisherman's Sweaters" and gasped when she turned over the price tag. She started to giggle when she thought that Micki would make some joke that the sweaters were phony — that it would probably take a Newfoundland fisherman a year to be able to afford one.

She was still thinking of Micki at the precise moment that she backed into someone. She wheeled in surprise to find that it wasn't just anyone, it was — Jonathan Brooks! He rocked back on his feet, adjusting his tortoiseshell glasses. She must have hit him harder than she had thought.

"Sorry," she muttered, wondering at the

strange fate that had brought them both to this store at this time.

"Quite all right," he said in that curious clenched-jaw voice. It was hard to believe that this was the boy Micki had rated number one on her cute list. Jonathan peered at her and his thin face lit up with recognition. "Ah, Susan," he said. "It's you."

Sarah frowned. "It's Sarah. Actually." She pronounced it "egg-shoo-ally," but the sarcasm was lost on him.

"What brings you here?" he said pleasantly.

"I was . . . out shopping," she told him, improvising. "What are you doing here?" she asked. Out of the corner of her eye, she noticed the salesman was giving her a funny look. With her windblown hair and her wrinkled windbreaker, she probably looked as out of place as a flamingo.

"Oh, I just came in to look at some sweaters." He began thumbing through a pile of "Genuine Australian Outback Explorer's Sweaters," and Sarah did some fast thinking. This was the perfect opportunity to put her plan into action. If Micki wanted Jonathan Brooks, she was going to do everything in her power to see that she got him. But how? There was no time for potions.

She'd had some success in the past with thought transference, not exactly mental telepathy, but something close. If she thought very, very hard, and if the other person's mind was open, sometimes she could plant a thought or idea there. The whole idea was to make the person think he had thought of it himself, and it took some skill.

Sarah was positive it would work in this case. Jonathan's mind seemed to be very open, in fact it seemed to be a blank, and she was sure that he would be receptive. She picked a point right behind his left ear and stared hard. Silently, she repeated Micki's name three times, and a few seconds later, Jonathan reached up absently to swat at that exact spot.

"Must be flies in here," he said, annoyed. Sarah was pleased. It was working perfectly.

Micki, she repeated silently. Call Micki Davis. This time she sent a mental picture of a telephone ringing, to give him an extra nudge.

"Did you hear something?" Jonathan said, whirling around suddenly.

"No, nothing," Sarah said innocently. She pretended to think. "Wait, I think I did hear a phone ringing someplace. Maybe in the background."

"That's good," Jonathan said, and then looked surprised. "I wonder why I said that?" Sarah stared at him and didn't answer. He wasn't bad-looking, she decided, her eyes taking in his broad shoulders and dark eyes. Of course, he was dressed like he was going to a preppy costume party — everything he wore had an alligator or an eagle plastered on it — but some girls seemed to like that.

"I don't know, why did you say that?" Sarah asked, fixing him with her brown eyes.

He ran his hand through his perfectly trimmed hair and gazed at the floor. "I don't know," he admitted. "Except . . . I'm glad they have a phone here because I just remembered I've got to call someone."

"Really?" Sarah spoke softly, afraid to spoil his concentration.

"Yes, that's it," he said, snapping his fingers. "I've got to call . . . Micki Davis. Do you happen to have her number?"

He certainly wasn't wasting any time, Sarah thought happily. She rattled off Micki's number by heart, and watched as he bolted toward the back of the store.

"Something for madame?" The salesman slithered close to her like a snake. "Perhaps something in safari clothes?"

"Afraid not," Sarah said. "I'm late for a cro-quet game," she said, darting to the front door. "But I'll be back — right after the salmon season."

It was very hard to keep her thoughts off Micki later that evening, and Sarah could hardly wait for dinner to be over so she could dash into her room and call her.

She amazed her parents by turning down a really terrific Spanish dessert, fried ice cream covered with whipped cream, and just made it to her room when the phone rang.

It was Micki. "Guess what?" Her voice was two octaves higher, shrieking over the lines.

"Haven't got a clue," Sarah said, clutching the phone to her ear and dropping into bed. She accidentally disturbed Bandit, her cat, and she quickly plumped up her bed pillow to make it up to him. He yawned and purred to show there were no hard feelings and promptly went back to sleep.

"You're not going to *believe* who just called me!"

"Try me," Sarah said wryly. She decided to play dumb, there was no sense in spoiling Micki's surprise.

"Jonathan Brooks." Micki paused as if she

had said the magic password, and in a way, she had, Sarah thought ironically.

"Jonathan Brooks," Sarah said vaguely. "Oh, yeah, I remember now. Cute, kind of preppy — "

"Kind of! He practically invented the word." Sarah could picture Micki, hugging her knees with excitement, her bright red hair tumbling around her face.

"I suppose he did," Sarah said, laughing. "Anyway, what did he want? A homework assignment or something?"

"No, that's just it," Micki said in an awed tone. "He called to ask me out. On a date," she added, in case Sarah hadn't understood.

"Why, Micki, I didn't know you two had a thing going."

"We didn't," Micki said. "Or at least, I didn't know we did. But he definitely wants to take me out. Me, Micki Davis! Can you believe it?"

"Of course I can believe it," Sarah said warmly. "Where are you going to go?"

"That's just it," Micki told her, and for the first time, Sarah thought her voice sounded a little different. Thinner and a little more . . . uptight? "Actually, he's leaving it up to me."

A tiny chill went through Sarah, but she brushed it aside. Micki had said "egg-shoo-ally" exactly the way Jonathan always said it. But that was crazy, impossible, unless it was some sort of unconscious imitation. Maybe that was it, Sarah decided. Micki had picked up one of Jonathan's speech patterns without even realizing it. No big deal.

"I'm really happy for you, Micki," she said. "Let's get together tomorrow and plan where you're going to go."

"Sounds super," Micki said feelingly.

Super? Sarah was getting worried. People who said "super" called the Beatles "The Fab Four."

"I'd better ring off now," Micki was saying. "See you tomorrow. Ta!"

Ta! Sarah slowly hung up the phone and turned to her dozing cat. "Bandit," she said softly, "I think I've done something wrong."

Chapter 4

Sarah knew she couldn't relax until she had a chance to see Micki in person, to talk about Jonathan's phone call. The next morning in school, she got right to the point.

"So, are you still pretty excited about going out with Jonathan Brooks?" Sarah kept her voice cheerful, but her heart sank as she noticed that Micki looked like she had just finished posing for an L.L. Bean catalog. She was wearing a tailored white blouse and a dark plaid kilt fastened with what looked like a giant gold diaper pin.

"Oh, yes," Micki said, and this time the nasal quality in her voice was unmistakable. "Egg-shoo-ally, I'm looking forward to it quite a bit." Sarah wondered briefly if all preppies had sinus problems.

The change in Micki was drastic, and Sarah knew that she was completely to blame. It involved more than just the new voice and the preppy clothes — although these would be the first things that people were going to notice — Micki's whole personality had changed. She seemed more distant, reserved, not the same old friend Sarah used to pal around with. Micki just didn't seem to be as much fun.

Jonathan Brooks wandered by just then and touched Micki lightly on the shoulder. "See you Friday," he said softly. Micki nodded coolly and turned back to Sarah. The old Micki would have been jumping up and down the minute Jonathan was out of sight, but the "new" Micki limited herself to a faint smile.

"So you're going to see him Friday night," Sarah said, trying to summon up some enthusiasm. "Hey, I've got a great idea. Why don't we go shopping today and buy you something terrific to wear?"

"That's an excellent idea," Micki agreed. Her voice was curiously flat, and Sarah sighed. This was all going to be uphill. A new worry crossed her mind. What if Micki didn't even *like* Jonathan Brooks? For that matter, she didn't seem to be particularly crazy over Sarah anymore. Or maybe preppies just didn't show emotion.

Maybe they were afraid it would wrinkle their perfectly pressed Polo shirts.

"Okay, that's settled, then," Sarah said quickly. "We'll go to the mall right after school and pick out something that's really dynamite. Then we'll go to Carmichael's and get one of those double-fudge sundaes you love. My treat." The sundae would be the test, Sarah decided. If she didn't go for that, she would be convinced that the real Micki had been abducted and replaced with this preppy imposter! "What do you say?" Sarah said eagerly, when Micki just stood there, staring blankly at her.

Micki opened her mouth slowly, as if choosing the right words was a great effort. A frosty smile hovered on her lips, and when she finally spoke, her tone wasn't reassuring. "I can hardly wait."

"I think Carousel is the best place to shop, don't you? They always have such a great selection, and the prices aren't bad." Sarah knew she was talking much too fast, but ever since they had arrived at the mall half an hour earlier, Micki had been strangely quiet. So Sarah had rambled on about denim miniskirts and silver doorknocker earrings, tired of hearing her own voice, and wondering where her best friend was hiding. Inside this cool preppy *person* you created, a little voice inside her head told her. When they turned a corner and reached Carousel, one of the trendier shops, Sarah practically had to push Micki inside.

"Was this where you wanted to go?" Micki said, finally finding her voice.

"Yes," Sarah babbled, licking her lips nervously. "Look at that great outfit on display. I love the way they've teamed that belted sweater up with those jeans and cowboy boots — "

"I don't think so."

"What?" Micki was already moving quickly toward the door, and Sarah had to jog to keep up with her. "What's wrong with it?" she demanded.

Micki smiled, a thin, superior smile that set Sarah's teeth on edge. "Nothing's *wrong* with it," she said patiently. Her voice was quiet and well-modulated. "I'm sure that certain . . . persons . . . would find those clothes . . . very appealing." Sarah waited for her to go on. "But it's not quite what I had in mind."

"But what did you have in mind?"

Another patient smile. "Something from Wooster's, I think."

"*Wooster's?*" For a moment, Sarah thought

she was kidding. None of her friends shopped at Wooster's. She doubted if even Eleanor Roosevelt would shop at Wooster's. The clothes came in two colors, taupish-gray, and grayish-taupe, and Sarah hated them both. They were boring, overpriced, and worst of all, they were made out of absolutely first-class materials that would never wear out.

"This is a joke, right?" The moment the words were out of her mouth, she realized her mistake. Preppies never joked.

"Hardly," Micki said icily. "If you'd rather not go with me — "

"No, I'll go, I'll go," Sarah said quickly. Her only hope was that Micki wouldn't find anything she liked at Wooster's, or that nothing would fit her.

Micki loved everything at Wooster's, and everything fit perfectly.

An hour later, spooning up double-fudge sundaes at Carmichael's — at least *that* hadn't changed, Sarah thought gratefully — Micki became more talkative.

"It's just so . . . amazing . . . that Jonathan and I never found each other before," she said, blotting her lips delicately. "We have so much in common, you know."

"You do?"

Micki nodded. "We spent hours on the phone last night, and I feel like I know him better than almost anyone in the world." Sarah felt a pang of jealousy at her words but tried not to show it. "We like the same books and movies, and he's taking me to a foreign film festival next Friday. He gets season tickets," she said proudly.

"That reminds me," Sarah said. "There's a great Godzilla movie on tonight. I thought I could tape it and we could watch it together on Saturday afternoon. It's one of the early ones, set in Tokyo." Sarah realized that something was terribly wrong. Micki was staring at her, her brown eyes wide with surprise.

"You want me to watch a Godzilla movie with you?" Her voice was incredulous.

Sarah's temper snapped. "Well, honestly, Micki, it's not like I'm asking you to spend the afternoon scrubbing floors. You *love* Godzilla movies." Or at least you used to, she added silently.

Micki opened her mouth to say something and then abruptly closed it. At least preppies are tactful, Sarah thought wryly. Micki scooped up the last of her sundae and took a long drink of water before replying. "Sarah," she said finally, "when I said I liked foreign films, Godzilla movies weren't quite what I had in mind." She stood up, checking herself in the mirror. "I really must dash," she said, throwing a plaid wool scarf around her neck. "Jonathan will be calling any minute."

Sarah reached for the check, and tried not to show how disappointed she felt. "Oh, in that case, I won't keep you," she said, imitating Micki's prissy accent. "Let's dash." Micki turned and gave her a sharp look, but Sarah smiled back innocently. She was already wondering what she could do to break the spell.

"It's your night for the dishes," Simon said happily that evening. His blond head was bent over the kitchen table as he studied a book of football plays.

"Okay," Sarah said absently. If Simon hadn't been sitting there, she would have used some of her magic powers to clean the kitchen. She filled the sink with soapy water and started to scrub the pans when the phone rang.

"It's for you," Simon yelled a moment later. "A *boy*!" He managed to convey the proper note of amazement and disbelief in his voice.

"Give me that," Sarah said impatiently. It must be Matt, calling about my biology notes, she thought. Wrong. It was David Shaw, a boy in her homeroom.

"Sarah," he said, his rich voice rumbling over the wires.

"David," she said, feeling pleased and giggly. "How are you?"

"I'm fine, now that I'm talking to the best-looking girl at Waterview High."

If anyone else had said that, Sarah would have groaned, but David Shaw was different. He could use the world's oldest lines — the world's corniest lines — and get away with it. She waited, wondering why he had called.

"Is this a bad time for you to talk?" he asked.

Sarah glanced at Simon, who was listening and pretending not to. If only she could send him someplace — like Antarctica — for a few minutes! She was careful not to formulate the thought as a *wish* because that was exactly what had gotten her in trouble before. Her wishes had a sneaky way of coming true, now that her magic powers were developing so quickly.

"No, this is fine." She looked at her reflection in the darkened kitchen window and saw that she was smiling. It was impossible not to smile around David. He had a voice that could melt the polar ice cap!

"I have a terrific idea," he said. "How would you like to go to a movie Friday night — "

"I'd love it," she said, interrupting him. So much for playing hard-to-get!

"And I'll throw in a pizza," he finished.

"Literally?"

He laughed, and Sarah immediately decided that there was one thing in the world better than his voice. It was his laugh. A lot of boys guffawed or snorted when they laughed — Matt had an unfortunate tendency to hiccup — but David's laugh was perfect. "Literally. I start working at the Pizza Palace Friday night, and my job is throwing pizzas."

"Throwing pizzas?" It sounded like a circus act, or something from *Star Search*.

"I'm exaggerating, but it's almost like that. You know the guys that wear the red-and-white-striped shirts and stand in the window twirling pizzas around? That's what I'll be doing."

"Wow," Sarah said, impressed. "Have you ever done that before?"

"Nope. But that's what makes it so exciting, right? If you've done something before, where's the challenge?"

Sarah thought hard. Something wasn't quite right. "David," she said slowly, "this is probably none of my business, but does your boss *know* you haven't done this before?"

"No, because that would spoil the fun."

"David," she said, suddenly worried, "I think you're letting yourself in for more than you can handle."

"I'm sure I can handle pizza dough," he teased her. "In fact, the whole secret is not to handle it too much, or it gets tough. Did you know that?"

"Yes. I mean, no," Sarah blurted out. She knew that Friday night was going to be a disaster. She could feel it.

"Look, meet me at the Pizza Palace at seven, and you'll have a chance to see me in action before we go to the movie. Bring a friend, if you like. I'll make sure you get some free pizza."

Nothing like being confident, Sarah thought. He hadn't even started working yet, and he was already arranging freebies for his friends.

"David — "

"See ya!" he said cheerfully and hung up.

When she hung up, Simon was looking at her with a curious expression. "You've got a date?" he said.

"That's right."

Simon did an elaborate pantomime of astonishment. He clutched his heart, leaned back in his chair, and opened his mouth wide. Then he suddenly sat straight up in his chair, winked, and gave her a thumbs-up sign. "Way to go, Sarah. Whoever he is, he's a lucky guy."

Sarah accepted the compliment graciously.

Chapter 5

A couple of days later, Sarah was sitting in French class, watching the hands move slowly on the big, old-fashioned wall clock. Time seemed to be frozen ever since David's phone call, and she wished that she could snap her fingers and suddenly find that it was Friday night. Unfortunately, changing time was *not* one of her magic powers, a fact that she had once proved to herself in a little experiment at Aunt Pam's.

So there was nothing to do but wait, she thought idly. She finished correcting her written assignment and glanced over at Micki, who was frowning at her paper. She hadn't seen Micki much this week, but it looked like nothing had changed. She was still the ultimate preppy. Today her friend was dressed in a heavy-ribbed sweater — a cream-colored knit that looked suspiciously like the ones at Rugby's — and soft leather moccasins. Knee socks, of course. Brand-new, but pre-faded to just the right shade of dusky charcoal.

She was still debating whether or not to undo the Jonathan Brooks spell, and now she promised herself to come to a decision soon. An immediate problem presented itself: She wasn't exactly sure *how* to undo the spell. She couldn't find the solution in any of the books she had read, and she didn't want to go to Aunt Pam and admit what she had done. She supposed that if she were absolutely desperate, she could stare at Jonathan's ear and mentally order him to "Dump Micki Davis," but that seemed pretty drastic. And it would certainly upset Micki. So it was a real dilemma, Sarah thought, chewing the end of her pencil.

"*C'est fini, mademoiselle?*" She hadn't heard Mme. Devereau approaching, and she was startled to see the teacher reaching for her paper.

"Uh, yes, I think so," Sarah said. Mme. Devereau frowned. She didn't like anyone to speak English in class when a simple French answer could be given.

To her horror, Mme. Devereau remained standing next to her desk, apparently deciding to correct her paper right on the spot. Whipping out a red felt-tip pen, she began making mad slashes over Sarah's paper, adding accent marks, crossing out verb endings, passionately underlining and circling everything in sight. And all the time, she was shaking her head disgustedly, and making "tut, tut, tut," sounds, but of course, she pronounced them with a French accent, so they sounded even more intimidating.

"C'est incroyable, absolument incroyable!" she said, slapping the paper on Sarah's desk. Allison Rogers snickered, but Mme. Devereau froze her with a look.

Sarah sank low in her seat, knowing enough French to realize that when Madame said her paper was "incredible, absolutely incredible," she didn't mean it as a compliment. In fact, just the opposite! Madame ordered Sarah to see her after class, and collected the rest of the papers, still shaking her head in amazement.

"I'll wait for you outside," Micki said, flashing her a sympathetic look when the class ended. So traces of the old Micki are still there, under that Izod exterior, Sarah thought happily.

Moments later, she was facing Mme. Devereau over the large oak desk. "Your grammar, punctuation, and spelling are appalling, Sarah, simply appalling," Madame said wearily. She permitted English outside of class, Sarah noticed, particularly if she was in the mood to lecture someone.

Sarah nodded, not bothering to disagree. She just couldn't seem to get the hang of French verb conjugations, and the tenses eluded her completely. Madame went over Sarah's mistakes, one by one, even though the next class was already filing in. "You're a bright girl, Sarah. I just can't imagine what the problem is."

"I'll try to do better on the next one," Sarah promised. She saw Micki out of the corner of her eye, waiting in the hall. The bell was going to ring any second, and Madame Devereau never gave anyone a late pass for the next class, even if she was the reason they were late.

"I sincerely hope so," Madame said sternly. "Remember, Sarah, this isn't a creative writing class. French grammar is not a matter of personal opinion — the rules have been codified for centuries." This was one of Madame's favorite speeches, and Sarah silently mouthed the words with her. "There are no shades of gray in French grammar, Sarah. Everything is in black and white."

"Black and white," Sarah murmured, finishing a second before Mme. Devereau did.

"What's that?"

"Uh, I said I'll be sure to see everything in black and white, Madame," Sarah said. "Starting right now." She turned, just as the bell rang, and met Micki in the hall. She knew why Micki looked worried. They would be late for basketball practice, and that meant an automatic detention.

"Hurry," Micki said urgently. "If we slip in the gym through the side door, Ms. James won't even know we're late." She pulled Sarah along with her, down the back steps that led to the locker room. "I'm really not in the mood to play basketball today, are you?" she asked, a couple of minutes later, pulling out a pair of faded blue gym shorts.

Only the shorts didn't look blue to Sarah. And Micki's hair didn't look bright copper anymore. Panicked, she squeezed her eyes tightly shut and opened them again.

Just as she thought. The scene danced before her eyes as though she were watching an old TV show. The lockers weren't pea-soup green, the concrete floor wasn't navy blue, her gym bag had lost its sunny yellow color.

Everything was in black and white.

Ms. James gave three short blasts on her whistle to signal everyone to come to order. They were divided into two teams — the Reds and the Blues — but as far as Sarah could tell, everyone was gray. She knew that she was a Red because she remembered she had been assigned a red T-shirt last week. And she remembered that Micki was a Red, too.

Outside of that, she was lost. It was going to be total chaos.

Before she knew what was happening, she was jostled onto the court with the rest of the girls, and practice had begun. Desperately, she stared at the sea of gray T-shirts, trying to recall who was who. There was no time to ask Micki, she'd have to rely on instinct.

Through an incredible stroke of bad luck, Micki immediately took possession of the ball and tried dribbling her way to the front, expecting Sarah to block out the Blues. But who was a Blue? Sarah stood by helplessly as Tina Jordan, moving like lightning, swept the ball right out from under Micki's outstretched palm. Micki shot her a look of surprise but bravely tried to grab the ball again. It was no use. Tina zigged and zagged her way to the goal, and with one fluid motion, sank a basket.

So Tina's a Blue, Sarah thought grimly. Now if she could just figure out who everyone else was! She stumbled her way through the rest of the first quarter, surprising and antagonizing everyone in sight. When Ms. James blew her whistle, Sarah retreated gratefully to the sidelines, with a worried Micki beside her.

"What was going on out there?" Micki hissed. "You let them get away with murder — " She was interrupted by a furious Allison Rogers who stormed over to tell Sarah that she needed glasses, and before Sarah could even reply, the game had started again.

Oh, no, here we go again, Sarah thought miserably. She shot Micki an apologetic look and tried to stay on the edge of the action. Her goal was to be as inconspicuous as possible, figuring that if she kept as far *away* from the ball as possible, she couldn't do any damage. This strategy worked perfectly until a few minutes later, when the ball practically dropped into her hands. Dribbling as hard as she could, her eyes darted wildly around the court until she spotted Micki.

Micki! she pleaded silently, and within seconds, her friend was at her side. Together they snaked their way closer and closer to the goal, until Sarah, leaping high in the air, sank the ball happily over the rim of the basket. When the whistle blew signaling the end of the practice, Sarah felt nearly giddy with relief.

"Are you okay?" Micki said later in the locker room. Sarah was suddenly overcome by a wave of dizziness and had stopped to rest her forehead on the cool metal of the locker door.

"I'm fine," she said with her eyes tightly shut. She waited a moment before she opened her eyes, hoping the locker door would be its familiar bile-green color.

So much for hoping. It was gray.

"That's super. You really had me worried there for a minute."

Super. Sarah felt a blanket of depression settle over her. Now that the excitement of the game was over, she realized that Micki's preppy personality was back, stronger than ever. Micki was pulling on her clothes, rambling on about the amazing and wonderful Jonathan Brooks, while Sarah dressed slowly, trying to figure out her next move.

"Well, I'd love to stay and chat, but I've got to meet Jonathan," Micki said cheerily. She tossed a pale blue cardigan over her shoulders, and knotted the sleeves carefully in the front, making sure that both ends were even. Sarah had never seen her do that before. Terminal preppyhood, she thought.

When Micki left the locker room, Sarah stopped to look at herself in the grimy mirror over the sink. Funny how you never picture yourself in black and white, she thought. Except in old photographs and maybe dreams. She picked up a strand of hair and let it fall limply to her shoulder. Without its chestnut-brown color, it looked dull and uninteresting, the way she felt. Her skin looked pale, and her features looked strangely flat, with no depth or contour. She could have sworn she wasn't wearing any lipstick, even though she had smeared on some pale peach gloss before French class.

I look awful, she thought. What will everyone think of me? Then she laughed grimly. Bizarre as it might seem, she only looked awful to *herself*! As far as everyone else could see, she was the same old Sarah.

She shrugged into her cherry-red (now charcoal) windbreaker and left the building, feeling depressed. What a week this has been, she thought. It was bad enough that her best friend had turned into a preppy, but now her whole world had turned gray! As usual, there was only one hope: Aunt Pam.

Plates and Pages was crowded when she arrived a few minutes later, but Aunt Pam took a moment to give her a cheery wave from behind the cash register. Sarah smiled and wandered down one of the narrow aisles. She loved the little store, with its endless rows of books and its collection of aromatic teas from all over the world. It was the perfect place to browse, and Sarah always found something interesting to read or sample. As soon as she could, Aunt Pam hurried over to her.

"What's up?" She kept her voice low, but it didn't matter, as there was a constant hum of conversation going on around them.

"I think I goofed," Sarah said ruefully. She quickly told her about Mme. Devereau, and her own promise to see everything in black and white. She stared closely at her aunt, wondering what she was wearing. She knew that her aunt had on a swirling caftan of some shimmery material, with a chunky metal necklace. Was it gold or silver? Sarah couldn't be sure. Darn it all, this was infuriating — she couldn't be sure of anything anymore!

"And you kept your promise," Aunt Pam said, trying not to smile. "Well, I told you that witches are always truthful. . . . You're a woman of your word, Sarah. I'm proud of you." Sarah knew that Aunt Pam was kidding, since her lips were twitching.

"Aunt Pam," she protested. "I don't want to keep my word, I want to see things again in color. Now will you help me or not?"

"Of course I'll help you," Aunt Pam reassured her. "I shouldn't have teased you," she added, giving her arm a light squeeze. "But you really didn't need to come to me. The problem will correct itself."

"It will?"

"Of course. If you can be patient."

"How patient?" Sarah said suspiciously. Aunt Pam's idea of time might be different from hers. What if she wanted her to be patient until she was thirty?

"Just until tonight." Aunt Pam laughed, a silvery sound that reminded Sarah of dozens of little china bells. "Have a good sleep tonight, and when you wake up the spell will be corrected," she said firmly.

Sarah sighed with relief.

"So which do you like?" Nicole asked Sarah half an hour later. She was holding up two identical sweaters.

"Is this a joke?" Sarah asked. She had dumped her books on the kitchen table, and was idly flipping through her algebra assignment. The nice thing about a math book, she thought, is that everything's in black and white! At least she knew she wasn't missing anything.

"Of course it's not a joke. I bought them at Brady's today, but I made sure I can bring one of them back." She held them up, one at a time, to her chest. "Which one goes best with my coloring?"

Sarah finally understood. "Oh!" she said, peering at the sweaters. She stood up to take a closer look, but naturally, it didn't do any good. "Gosh, it's hard to say. This will take some thought."

"Honestly, Sarah, I'm not asking you to figure out the budget deficit," her sister said impatiently. "Just tell me which one you like the best. I want to wear one tonight." Nicole lifted up both sweaters and tucked them under her chin.

"Um . . . I think the one on the right," Sarah said hesitantly.

"My right or your right?"

"Uh . . . my right." Sarah tried to scurry back to her math book, but Nicole wasn't satisfied.

"But I hardly ever wear pink," she complained.

As a future fashion designer, Sarah knew right away that pink was a terrible color for Nicole to wear. Cool blues and greens were much more flattering to Nicole's blonde good looks.

"I didn't mean my right," Sarah said brightly. "I meant your right."

"Oh," Nicole said. "Well, that's different." She looked at the sweater carefully, running her hand over the little lace collar. Sarah was dying to know what color it was, and wondered how she could ask.

"I really like it, and it will go with a lot of things," Sarah added. She was betting it was robin's-egg-blue or sea-green, two of Nicole's favorite colors.

"So you really think I should keep this one?"

Nicole was already cutting off the price tags.

"I really do," Sarah said enthusiastically. "It was made for you."

"That's what the saleslady said," Nicole said. "But I wanted to check with you, just to make sure. After all, you're the fashion expert." Sarah beamed and tried to look modest.

"And if you say pumpkin is my color, Sarah, that's good enough for me."

Dazed, Sarah went back to her algebra book. Pumpkin? She had just persuaded her sister to buy a pumpkin sweater? She decided to go to bed right after dinner. It was the only way she could be sure she wouldn't make any more mistakes.

Chapter 6

"I feel a little silly, tagging along like this," Micki said the following Friday night. She and Sarah were sitting at a back booth in the Pizza Palace, waiting for Tina and Heather to show up.

"Why?" Sarah asked, surprised. "David said I could bring some friends. Anyway, it's just for an hour. David's getting off work at eight so we can go to the movies."

Sarah hadn't spent much time with Micki in the past week and she leaned across the table, saying impulsively, "Look, are you sure you and Jonathan don't want to come with us?"

Micki shook her head. "Jonathan's already made plans for us to go to the foreign film festival. I told him to meet me here at seven-thirty." She looked serious, as if she had something on her mind. "Uh, Sarah," she began, "there's something I have to tell you. Jonathan thinks . . . I mean, I think . . . that it's about time I did something with my name."

"Your name?" Sarah looked blank. "What would you do with it?"

"Change it," Micki said flatly. "You know it's never really been right for me."

"Never been right for you? You've been Micki forever," Sarah objected. "I'm surprised you'd want to go back to being Michelle." Sarah was shocked. First the voice, then the clothes, now the name! What was going to be next?

"Oh, I'll never use Michelle." Micki laughed. "I dropped that in kindergarten. It's simply awful." She paused and sipped her cola. "Jonathan . . . and I . . . thought of this really peachy new name for me, and I want everyone to start using it."

"What is it?" Sarah said, fearing the worst. Her mind raced through a list of possible preppy names. Cissy, Buffy. . . .

"Muffin," Micki said.

"Muffin!" Sarah was so startled, she nearly dropped her drink into her lap. Muffin wasn't the name for a best friend. It was the name for a cocker spaniel. She put the glass carefully on the table before she trusted herself to speak again.

"That's right," Micki said happily. "Jonathan thought of it himself."

"How clever of him," Sarah murmured, dabbing at her lace blouse with her napkin. A few stray dots of cola were splattered on the sleeves, and she wondered if they would stain.

"Yes, he is, isn't he?" Micki was beaming. "And the nice thing about it is that it can be shortened to Muffy. But just for special friends, like you," she added generously. "Jonathan says that if everyone starts using your nickname, it's not special anymore, so it's not even worth having."

"I always knew that Jonathan was full of . . . clever ideas," Sarah said.

"Oh, he is! He says. . . ."

Jonathan's latest sayings were lost forever because Tina and Heather reached the table at the exact same moment that David dashed out from the kitchen.

"Sorry to keep you waiting," he said. "I saw you come in a little while ago, but we were backed up with orders." David looked like he had just escaped from a barbershop quartet. He was wearing a peppermint-striped shirt with a stiff white collar, a pair of black pants, and a red satin armband. Sarah had no idea what the armband was for, but she knew one thing: He looked absolutely adorable!

Tina and Heather slid into the booth, and wriggled out of their coats. A waitress placed a steaming pizza on the table, and David beamed. "My treat."

"I'm glad everybody could make it tonight," he said. He tore his gaze away from Sarah long enough to glance around the table. "I wish I could sit down with you guys, but I'd better run. My big moment is coming up, so wish me luck, okay?" His voice was low and husky and he had a way of looking at Sarah as though she were the only girl in the room.

"Your big moment?" Sarah asked.

"It's time for me to do my show in the window — you know, twirling pizzas in the air, dazzling the crowds." He smiled to show he wasn't taking it seriously.

Sarah felt a knot of fear in the pit of her stomach. "But David, are you sure you'll be okay?" She had the horrible feeling that something awful was going to happen, just like in one of those horror movies. He'd pick up the pizza dough, creepy music would start to play, something with strings in a minor key, and then. . . .

The image dissolved when David got up from the table. "Of course I will. Besides, it sure beats standing in the kitchen chopping anchovies."

As soon as he left, Heather and Tina turned to her, and said in unison, "He's *darling*!"

"You've been keeping secrets," Tina said.

"This is the first time I've gone out with him," Sarah insisted. "He's in my homeroom, but I had no idea he even noticed me. You can ask Micki. I mean Muffin. That's what she wants to be called."

Tina turned to Micki. "What's this Muffin business? It makes you sound like a Twinkie."

Sarah watched while Micki fumbled a little, trying to explain about Jonathan and his "great ideas." She could see from Tina's raised eyebrows that she wasn't buying any of it, and Heather looked equally skeptical.

"Sounds like he's trying to do one of those magazine make-overs on you," Tina objected. "First the clothes," she said, her eyes running over Micki's skirt and blouse, "and now your name!"

When Micki stood up to get change for the

jukebox a moment later, Tina made her position clear. "Look, Sarah," she said firmly. "You're Micki's best friend, so I think you should know that a lot of the kids are making fun of her."

"Making fun of Micki?" Sarah felt color flood into her cheeks.

"That's right," Tina said. "I don't want to hurt her feelings, but I thought maybe you could talk to her, you know, do something."

"You could try to get her to give up this crazy preppy act," Heather suggested. "We thought it was a gag at first, but it seems to be for real."

"It's for real, all right," Sarah admitted. "Micki has changed her whole style." But it's not her fault, she added to herself. It's mine.

"Please, Sarah," Heather said, as Micki made her way back to the table, "do something before it's too late!"

Sarah murmured that she would do her best, but her attention was taken up by a new problem: David had donned a butcher's apron, and was now preparing to take his place in the front window of the Pizza Palace. Sarah tried to quiet the feeling of apprehension that washed over her. There's absolutely nothing to worry about, she said silently. He'll probably be terrific at this. David certainly seemed confident, she admitted, as he poked and prodded the huge mound of sticky dough, finally dividing it into three portions the size of snowballs.

"I think he's going to flip the dough up in the air like that other guy did," Tina said, half-rising out of her seat to watch. "They say they do it to make the dough fluffy or something, but I think they just like to put on a show."

David is enough of a show, all by himself, Sarah thought. She looked at his gleaming black hair, his handsome profile, his terrific green eyes. She wanted the evening to be perfect, special, a night neither of them would ever forget.

Her heart skipped when David smiled enchantingly at the small crowd that had gathered outside the front window of the restaurant. He began to toss the dough back and forth in his hands, from left to right, right to left, like a juggler. He was being careful not to toss the dough too high, Sarah noticed, so there weren't any slip-ups. After a minute or so of this, she saw him hesitate, as if wondering what to do next. He clearly hadn't a clue how to begin spinning the dough in the air, and the crowd was starting to drift away.

That's when it came to her: She could help

him! She concentrated as hard as she could, and suddenly the dough seemed to come to life. An amazed look passed over David's face as the dough suddenly soared high in the air, making a graceful arc as he changed it from hand to hand. And another strange thing happened: The dough seemed to be feather-light, so light it barely touched his palm before whizzing through the air again and again. Sarah saw that a few people who had turned away were drifting back, and now they were smiling and pointing at him.

"Look at that!" Tina said admiringly. "David's really got them going."

Sarah didn't dare take her eyes off David — she was afraid of losing her concentration. Now was the time to try something big, something really dramatic, that would assure his future at the Pizza Palace forever. David gave her the perfect opportunity right then, because he started to rotate the dough, stretching and thinning it, until it was flattened into a disk the size of a Frisbee. Once Sarah realized what he was doing, she concentrated as hard as she could to help him. Now he was ready to twirl the dough into the air, she decided. This was the ideal moment.

She squeezed her eyes tightly shut, and

when she had opened them, the dough was spinning and soaring like a glider plane. She heard Heather and Tina gasp beside her, but nothing would make her look away from David. The white disk of dough defied gravity as it zoomed almost to the ceiling, spinning madly, and then landed perfectly in David's out-stretched hands. David looked surprised and excited. This will keep them talking for years, Sarah thought.

She decided to keep the dough airborne a little longer, so it hovered near the ceiling fan like a flying saucer, before returning gently to earth. People inside were deserting their pizzas to catch the show at the window. Even the cook, who had rushed out from the kitchen in his chef's hat, gaped in surprise.

Sarah kept the pizza dough in the air long enough for David to fold his floury arms in front of his chest and take a deep bow, before letting it settle gently in his hands once more. A second later, it swooped off again, twisting and soaring like a kite as it neared the ceiling, and then spinning madly for ten seconds. Sarah felt giddy with power as a gasp went up from the crowd. It was a magical moment, a moment she would never forget. Never had she felt so sure of herself, so proud of her powers. David's smiling face, the cheering crowd, the soaring dough — all this would be etched in her mind forever.

And then Heather spilled her drink in Sarah's lap.

For a moment, everything stopped, like one of those freeze-frame pictures on television, and then three things happened simultaneously. Heather wailed an apology, Sarah glanced down, wondering why her lap was suddenly filled with ice cubes, and a loud noise from the crowd filled her ears.

Dimly, she realized that the crowd wasn't cheering anymore, they were laughing. And not just chuckling, but laughing hysterically! The people in the aisle had shifted, blocking her view, and she frantically pushed Heather aside to get a look. Her eyes swept the room, and everywhere she saw people nearly bent over double with laughter. What in the world had happened?

And then she saw David.

No longer the confident showman, David was standing in the front window, his head covered in pizza dough. He was trying to fight his way out of the soggy mess, but it was almost impossible. Long strands of the dough trailed down his neck and shoulders, and the more he tried to extricate himself, the worse it got.

Oh, no, Sarah breathed. She ignored Heather, who was still trying to dab at her pants with a napkin, and half-rose out of the booth. Concentrating as hard as she could, she willed the pizza dough to immediately roll itself back up in a neat ball and sit on the counter.

Amazingly, it did, and a dazed-looking David appeared from underneath. He looked shaken, but okay, and Sarah breathed a sigh of relief.

"Wow, how'd he do that?" Tina asked.

"Okay folks, the show's over," the cook said, waving everyone back to their booths. The crowd inside slowly dispersed, talking in small groups, shaking their heads as if they weren't quite sure what they had just seen.

All except David. He stood rooted to the spot, with a blank expression on his face. He looked like he had been struck by lightning, and Sarah's heart turned over.

Oh, David, she thought. What have I done to you?

Chapter 7

"It wasn't that bad," David said earnestly to her a couple of hours later. "In fact, it was really kind of funny." They had stopped for a quick hamburger at Carmichael's; David said he wanted nothing to do with pizza for the next five years or so — and then had hurried to catch the movie at the Strand.

Sarah thought that David looked really handsome in the half-lit movie theater, as they waited for the movie to begin. She wondered if he would want to hold hands with her, and decided not to have any buttered popcorn — her favorite — just in case.

"You're really being a good sport about it. A lot of people wouldn't have been able to carry it off the way you did," she said.

David grinned. "Well, when the pizza dough

hit me in the head, I figured I had two choices. I could either laugh it off, or go throw myself in a vat of spaghetti sauce." He paused, and leaned a little closer to her. "I don't look too good covered with tomatoes and garlic."

Sarah laughed with him. She had been speechless with horror at the scene in the window, but David had played up the moment for all it was worth, smiling and bowing at the crowd, cheerfully announcing that he would give a repeat performance the following evening. Somehow he had made it seem like a wonderful gag, managing to turn things around, so the customers thought it was all part of the act.

Sarah had said very little, trying to figure out her own role in the disaster. It was the spilled drink that did it, she decided. As long as she concentrated, keeping all her energies focused on David, everything had been fine, but once she got distracted, things had fallen apart. A good lesson for an apprentice witch, Aunt Pam would say.

"I still can't figure it out," David was telling her. "You know, for a while there, I was really on a roll. I was beginning to think I might make the *Guiness Book of World Records* for spinning pizza dough." He surprised her by reaching for her hand. Sarah sighed and looked at the screen. And then she gasped aloud, like someone had punched her in the stomach.

Everything was black and white. Again.

"What's wrong?" David asked softly.

She turned to face him in the dark. "The movie. . . ." She stopped herself just in time. She could never tell David about the spell.

David looked puzzled. "I thought you said you liked Woody Allen."

"I do, but — "

"*Manhattan* is one of my favorites," David went on. Sarah saw out of the corner of her eye that the opening credits were rolling. "I think the black-and-white photography adds a lot, don't you? It really gives you the feel of the city."

"Black-and-white photography?" Sarah repeated.

David nodded. "He's only made two movies in black and white, and they've both been very popular." He had stopped talking, and was giving her a strange look. Sarah made an effort to pull herself together. "Are you sure nothing's wrong?" His voice was low.

"Everything's fine," Sarah whispered, nearly giddy with relief. The movie was filmed in black and white! The spell hadn't come back, there was nothing to worry about. "Really."

"In that case, I'll be right back," David said. He dropped her hand and slid out of his seat. "I'm going to get us two of the biggest tubs of popcorn they have. Buttered, of course."

"Of course," Sarah said weakly.

Sarah spent the last half of the movie wondering how the evening would end, and felt a little nervous about saying good-night to David at the door. Would he kiss her? Did boys worry about things like that, too?

She remembered reading somewhere that seventy-five percent of the things people worry about going wrong never even happen, and kissing David at the door was the perfect example. It just happened so naturally, she barely had time to react when his lips brushed hers. They had been walking home hand in hand, talking about everything from books to UFO's, when they suddenly reached her front porch.

"I had a great time," David said softly. He moved in close to her, smiling, and Sarah was wondering what to say to him. He had taken the words right out of her mouth! She didn't have to wonder for long, though, because the next thing she knew, they nearly bumped noses as he bent to kiss her. She moved a millimeter to the right just in time, and everything went smoothly.

"So did I," Sarah managed to say, when he drew back to look at her.

"Hey, I've got an idea," he said.

"You do?" She wondered why she sounded so breathless.

David nodded. "Why don't we do this again? Everything except the pizza dough falling on my head," he teased.

"You want to go out again?" Sarah asked, dazed. This is perfect, she thought, and I haven't even had to use my powers to pull it off.

"How about next Friday night?"

"Great," Sarah said, and practically floated in the front door. What a night — what a wonderful, fantastic night! A kiss, and he wanted to see her again. She raced to her room, all set to call Micki, and then stopped, remembering. Micki was out somewhere with Jonathan — probably watching a movie with subtitles — and would be so preppy and cool, she wouldn't be any fun to talk to.

Sarah flopped on her bed, and a moment later, Bandit landed with a heavy thud on her pillow. It was definitely time to do something about Jonathan, she thought, running her hand over Bandit's thick fur. She'd have to do it very carefully, very subtly, so Micki never suspected why he was breaking up with her. She paused, thinking, and she spotted her notebook on the floor. Her mind flew back to the day she had asked Micki to rate the boys in the cafeteria.

Of course! She'd go on to number two on the list, Jeff Tyson, wasn't it? She'd cancel the spell on Jonathan, and then Jeff could fall in love with Micki. He was sort of a jock, but he was *bound* to be an improvement on Jonathan, and at least Micki would go back to being her old self again. She knew she'd better do it fast. Micki was becoming more preppy by the minute, and if word got around school that she was calling herself "Muffin," she'd never live it down!

Maybe she could call Jeff right now, she thought. If he was home on a Friday night, that would be really encouraging, and would probably mean he wasn't dating anyone. She hunted in the desk for her Waterview student directory, and dragged it over to the bed. She wasn't sure how to handle the phone call — after all, she barely knew Jeff Tyson — and was staring into space when Simon poked his head around the door.

"Want some tea? Nicole's making some."

"Sure, I — " She stared at Simon, and then it hit her. Simon was a jock, Jeff was a jock, they spoke the same language. She decided to take a chance. "Simon, I need your advice on something."

"Shoot." He lounged in the doorway, his lanky figure filling the frame.

"I . . . uh, I mean, a friend of mine . . . wants to get to know Jeff Tyson. What would you suggest?"

"What would I suggest?" Simon touched the ceiling like he were shooting an imaginary basket, then landed lightly on the balls of his feet.

"She needs an excuse to call him, or to see him," Sarah explained. "Can you think of something?"

Simon frowned in thought. "That's a tough one."

He snapped his fingers and said, "Here it is." He spread his large hands expansively. "The perfect excuse. You know Joe Dominick, the captain of the hockey team?"

"I know who he is. Go on."

"Well, Joe and I have Civics together."

"And — "

"And he told me he's got to call every single

guy on the team and say that Saturday's game is going to be delayed by an hour. Instead of meeting at one, they're going to meet at two." Simon looked pleased with himself. "So all your friend has to do is call up and say she's calling for Joe — she can pretend she's his mother or something — and deliver the message. How's that?"

Sarah jumped off the bed excitedly. "It's perfect. Just what I'm looking for."

"Hello, could I speak to Jeff, please?" Sarah said a few minutes later. She had rehearsed her speech over and over but she still felt nervous.

"This is Jeff," a hearty voice answered.

Sarah took a deep breath and launched into her speech. "Well, I'm calling for Joe Dominick," she said brightly.

"Joe Dominick? Yeah?"

"Yes, that's right. And I just want to tell you that Saturday's game will be delayed one hour. From one to two." She waited a beat and then concentrating as hard as she could, she murmured, "Call Micki Davis. Ask her out." Her voice was low, barely above a whisper. She had no idea if he would take the suggestion or not, but she didn't dare repeat it.

There was a dead silence, and then Jeff said suspiciously, "Who is this?"

Sarah froze. How had he caught on? She tried mentally sending him the same message. *Call Micki Davis*, she pleaded silently. *Call Micki Davis*. She was so nervous, she nearly dropped the receiver. Darn it all, it had to sink into Jeff's thick skull — it just had to!

"I said, who is this?"

"Have a nice day!" Sarah said breezily. She slammed the receiver down, and sat shaking for a moment. Her heart was hammering so fast, she thought her chest would explode. She had never tried sending a mental message over the phone before, and she had no idea if the message would go through, or if Jeff would accept it. Maybe Jeff was less receptive than Jonathan, maybe it was a mistake to even try to cast a spell on him. Then she thought of Micki, who was probably going to ruin her life by changing her name to Muffin. No, she *had* to step in and do something. On Monday, she'd cancel the spell she put on Jonathan, and make sure that the new spell on Jeff was in place.

On Monday, everything would work out.

Chapter 8

Monday morning was a disaster.

Sarah overslept, and when Nicole finally rapped on her door, it was already past seven-thirty. Sarah tumbled out of bed with a start, and still clutching her quilt around her, dashed to the shower. A quick blast of cold water — no time to wait for the temperamental water heater to come to life — and she was back in her room, rummaging in her closet.

Of all the days to be late! she thought, ferreting through her wardrobe. She wanted to wear something terrific, something so dazzling that David Shaw wouldn't be able to take his eyes off of her.

She yanked a corduroy skirt off a hanger, remembered that the zipper was broken, and tossed it on the floor. "Jeans," she said frantically. "When in doubt, wear jeans." She pulled out her best pair of faded Levi's, wriggled into them, and added a white shaker-knit sweater. It wasn't the most exciting outfit she had ever put together, but maybe if she added a pair of cowboy boots, and that gold necklace Micki had given her, she'd be okay.

Micki. She had to tackle that problem today, she thought. She made a mental note: The moment she got to school, she'd plan her attack on Jonathan Brooks.

She took another look at the clock. Just enough time to run a brush through her tangled chestnut hair and dab on some peach lip gloss. She flew into the kitchen, scooped up her history term paper off the kitchen table, and was almost out the door when she collided with Simon.

The next few seconds seemed to happen in slow motion, like an instant replay. Everything was clear, razor-sharp, and frozen in time. Her brain registered every detail: Simon's slow smile as he turned from the refrigerator, Nicole's scream, the freshly typed term paper, clutched tightly to her chest, and worst of all, the giant pitcher of orange juice that was coming right at her! She knew without a doubt what was going to happen, but was powerless to stop it. She could see the juice splashing over the edge of the pitcher, leaving a wet trail over her sweater, her shoes, and of course, her history paper.

She closed her eyes, and a millisecond later, it all came true. Simon jumped back just in time, so Sarah got the full force of the juice. "Simon!" she began furiously, and then stopped. It was too late to be angry, she thought. It was too late to do anything but pick up her soggy papers and run out the door.

Her mother came in the kitchen just then, glanced at the clock and said sharply, "Sarah, hurry up. You'll be late for school."

That was the last straw. "Late for school? Late for school!" Sarah shouted. She sputtered, wiping away a piece of orange pulp that had landed on her chin. Her clothes were stained, her paper was drenched, her day was ruined. And her mother was talking about *school*? Then Sarah said the words that she would regret a dozen times, the words that would rock Waterview and change the course of their lives.

"I wish the stupid school would just disappear!"

Seven minutes later, Sarah darted across Union Street, and then raced around the corner at Fifth and Spruce. She'd made the trip in record time, even though she was out of breath, and her hair was clinging damply to her neck. So much for impressing David Shaw, she thought. She took a last despairing look at her term paper, which was turning a mottled yellow color under her arm, and ducking her head against the brisk wind, sprinted the last half block to school.

Funny, she thought, there were quite a few kids late to school this morning. She must have made better time than she realized, or else the first bell hadn't even rung yet. That would be a stroke of luck, she decided. Thinking quickly, she planned her strategy. Maybe she could see Jonathan before homeroom, and zap him with a mental message to dump Micki. Then she could find Jeff Tyson, just to make sure the spell she had cast over the phone had really worked. That would be one big problem solved before the day even started.

Ignoring the excited buzz of conversation around her, she headed for the front steps of the school, and came to a screeching halt.

There were no steps.

Impossible. She staggered backwards, still holding her paper, and tried to focus her eyes. What was going on? She stared at her feet as if they were playing a trick on her. What were they doing on this patch of brown dirt? They should be running up seventeen buff-colored concrete steps right this minute, she thought. Suddenly she realized that the voices behind her sounded different this morning. They were shocked, high-pitched, some even a little panicky.

She raised her eyes slowly from her shoes, her heart thudding. Then she caught her breath. The sight in front of her was so incredible that her brain rebelled.

She was looking at a vacant lot. The school was gone!

"What do you think — is this exciting or what?" She turned slowly as Heather Larson bobbed up next to her.

"What's going on?" Sarah asked weakly. "What happened to the school?" Her mouth was so dry, she could hardly force the words out. She longed to sit down, but that was out of the question — the low concrete wall was gone, too.

"Who knows?" Heather smiled broadly and threw up her hands. "I guess one minute it was here, and the next minute — poof! — it was gone. No one knows what to make of it, but I know one thing."

"What's that?" Sarah said. Her eyes moved over the crowd, but there was no sign of Micki. Somehow she felt it was very important to see her best friend, maybe together they could make sense of this.

"We won't have school today, that's for sure! It's out of sight!" Heather giggled happily, as if it were all a wonderful joke. Then she frowned. "Unless somebody figures out a way to get it back." She tapped Sarah's arm. "You don't think they will, do you? I have a French test today, and I didn't get a chance to study."

"Heather, please, I'm trying to think." Sarah brushed Heather's hand away while her mind raced over the possibilities. She was positive that she had caused the school to disappear. She had literally wished it away! But the question now was, what could she do to bring it back?

She stared at the scene around her, trying to calm herself. They were standing in the middle of a huge vacant lot, and there was absolutely nothing to indicate that it used to be the site of a high school. The dirt under their feet was firmly packed, dark brown, and looked as if it had been undisturbed for years. But of course that's what you would expect, Sarah thought. The school building has been sitting on top of it all this time. A few soda cans and gum wrappers littered the edges of the lot, but that was all. It was the strangest sight she had ever seen.

Sarah suddenly thought of something — the playing field! There would be football goals, bleachers, yards and yards of green grass. She ran a few feet to the right and stopped in confusion. The playing field should be to the left, just behind the school, but she couldn't see a trace of it. She ran back to Heather, when Matt Neville stopped her.

"It's gone, too," he said gently. "The playing field, the clubhouse, the softball diamond — everything. It's a mystery," he said thoughtfully. "The teachers don't seem to know any more than we do, and I've heard that the principal is so freaked out, he's asked the governor to call the National Guard."

Sarah recognized a lot of teachers in the crowd, along with some of her friends' parents, who drove carpools.

"The National Guard! You mean, like on television?" Heather cried. She immediately fluffed her blonde hair, and glanced around self-consciously. "Well, just between us, I have my own theory about what happened."

"You do?" Matt and Sarah turned to her in surprise.

She leaned close and said in a low voice, *"Candid Camera."*

"What?" Sarah couldn't believe it.

"Candid Camera," Heather repeated softly. "You know, that old TV show where they play a trick on you, and they film the whole thing. It's all a joke, don't you get it?" She waved her slim arm at the empty lot. "Any minute, someone's going to jump out of a van and say, 'Smile, you're on *Candid Camera!*' "

"I don't think so, Heather," Matt said patiently. "Look around. It's no trick. The school really is gone."

"It just *looks* gone," Heather said stubbornly. Her blue eyes were bright with excitement, and Sarah realized that she was enjoying the whole thing. Didn't Heather understand that a lot of people were going to be very upset? she thought. Plus what if the school never came back? What would they do then?

Heather explained her theory to Matt. "The way I see it," she was saying, "is that they did it all with mirrors. Sort of like David Copperfield and the Statue of Liberty."

"Heather," Matt said, shaking his head. "That was television. This is real life. Look. You can prove it to yourself. You can walk right through the empty space here."

"Talk about a surprise," a preppy voice said. Sarah turned in relief as Micki joined them. Micki looked cool and poised in a pale blue blouse and a pair of tailored charcoal pants. It would take more than a disappearing school to shake up a preppy, Sarah thought.

"Micki, are you all right?" Sarah asked anxiously. She was so glad to see her, she wanted to throw her arms around her, but she knew this would embarrass the "new" Micki.

"Of course I'm all right, why wouldn't I be?" Micki asked. She tied the belt on her trench coat, automatically making sure the sides were exactly the same length.

"Well, I don't know. This whole thing is so . . . scary," Sarah said feelingly. "I mean, you come to school, and find yourself staring at a vacant lot."

Micki have her a patronizing smile. "It wouldn't be the end of the world if Waterview disappeared forever, you know."

"Micki!" Sarah was astonished.

"Don't look so shocked," Micki went on in

her new preppy voice. She was infuriatingly calm, and she picked a nonexistent piece of lint off her trench coat. "I don't know about you," she said, including Matt and Heather, "but I've been simply dying to transfer to Fairmont, and this would be the perfect opportunity."

"Fairmont?" Matt asked, raising his eyebrows. Fairmont was the most expensive private school in town.

"Wouldn't it be wonderful?" Micki asked, her voice slipping into a dreamy tone. "They actually wear uniforms, you know. The boys wear white shirts and burgundy ties, and the girls wear those darling little pleated skirts."

"Micki, I can't believe this," Sarah blurted out. Here they were, in the middle of the biggest disaster of their lives, and Micki was talking about pleated skirts! The first chance she got, she was going to find Jonathan Brooks and end this preppy monster forever!

"I've even heard that golf is part of their PE courses," Heather volunteered. Sarah wanted to strangle her.

"That's true," Micki agreed. "And there's archery and fencing. . . ."

Sarah tuned out, trying to figure out what to do next. It was obvious that she wasn't going to solve anything hanging around the school-yard. It was already jammed with students and teachers, and from the wail of sirens in the distance, it sounded like the police would be there any minute. And no one was *doing* anything, she thought. Most of the kids looked shocked, and the teachers seemed too dazed to offer any advice. Everyone was talking at once, not really listening to anything anyone else was saying, and the whole scene was giving Sarah a giant headache.

She picked up part of Micki's conversation and shook her head in disgust.

"You see," Micki was saying in that uptight way, "if Waterview is gone forever, my parents will *have* to send me to Fairmont."

"We'll all have to find a new school," Heather pointed out. For once, she was being logical.

"That's true," Micki said slowly. It was obvious she hadn't thought of that. "Of course, if a lot of you wanted to go to Fairmont, that would be a problem."

"Why's that?" Matt asked.

Micki gave a superior little smile. "Fairmont is a very special place, Matt. And if *everyone* wanted to go there" — she paused and fluttered her hands — "well, as Jonathan always says, it just wouldn't be special anymore."

Sarah had heard enough. She backed slowly away from the group, sure that she wouldn't be missed in all the confusion. There was only person on the face of the earth who could get her out of this mess: Aunt Pam.

Chapter 9

Plates and Pages was closed on Monday mornings, but Aunt Pam welcomed Sarah into her bright apartment above the shop.

"I just heard it on the news," she said, her golden eyes looking searchingly at her niece. "They said that Waterview High is gone. Can it be true?"

"It's true all right," Sarah said wearily. She dropped into an overstuffed white chair and glanced around the living room. It was light and airy, the handmade oak furniture piled high with colorful cushions. Usually Sarah felt relaxed the moment she stepped inside her aunt's home, but today nothing could cheer her up. She closed her eyes for a moment, and when she opened them, she caught Aunt Pam staring at her sympathetically.

"How did it happen?" her aunt said softly. She poured Sarah a steaming cup of hot chocolate from a stoneware pitcher on the coffee table.

She knows, Sarah thought. "I wished it to happen . . . and it happened." She paused. "It was a terrible accident. I was having a bad morning, and the words just popped out before I could stop them." She explained about Simon and the orange juice, remembering that she was still holding her soggy term paper in her lap.

Her aunt listened carefully, shaking her head from time to time. She looked beautiful even in the morning, Sarah thought. She was wearing a wine-colored robe that reached to her ankles. She was wearing no makeup, and she had swept her jet-black hair into a thick braid that tumbled over one shoulder.

"I think the first thing we need to do is assess the damage," Aunt Pam said thoughtfully.

"What do you mean?"

"Well, there's so much we don't know. For example, is the school really lost, or is just misplaced? And was it empty when it disappeared, or were there some people inside?"

"I never even *thought* of that," Sarah admitted. What if there *were* people inside! she thought, shocked. She might have made some of her friends disappear.

"Until we have the answers to those questions, we can't possibly decide on a course of action. Perhaps the first thing we should do is — wait a minute, they're talking about it right now." She broke off suddenly and stared at the television. It was on, Sarah noticed, but the volume was lowered. Aunt Pam blinked once, and immediately, the volume went up and the voice of Deborah Dodds, a local television reporter, filled the room. She was standing in a vacant lot, holding a microphone, smiling brightly at the camera.

Suddenly Sarah recognized a giant elm tree in the background and leaned forward. "That's Waterview!" she said excitedly. "Or at least it used to be."

"The big news this morning is the strange disappearance of Waterview High. It's 'now you see it, now you don't time,' " Deborah was saying in her perkiest voice, "and everybody is just baffled. We're here on the scene, and as you can see, the school isn't." Deborah flashed a dazzling smile, chuckling a little at her own joke. The camera pulled back to reveal groups of happy students milling around, laughing and shouting, as teachers tried to restore order.

"Let's see if we can get a few comments from the Waterview kids," Deborah was saying. She plunged into the crowd as the camera followed her. "Hi, there," she said cheerily. The crowd opened, and Sarah saw that Heather Larson had managed to position herself right in front of the camera. "Well, you look like a typical Waterview student." Heather smiled prettily with her hands folded in front of her. "How does it feel to be out of school?"

"What does she mean out of school!" Sarah said. "You'd think it was a holiday!"

Heather thought for a moment. "Well, it's kind of fun to have a day off, but we're all pretty surprised at what happened."

Deborah nodded encouragingly, as if Heather had just said something profound. "Having your school disappear would be pretty surprising, I'm sure" — she glanced at the camera — "but do you have any idea what happened here?"

Heather was stumped. She tossed her blonde hair a little so it fell over her shoulders, and looked directly into the camera. "Gosh, no. There are some theories, but nothing really definite."

"Theories?" The reporter looked interested. "What sort of theories?"

"Well, I sort of figured it was one of those *Candid* — "

"UFO's," someone called out from the back of the crowd. "Aliens from outer space. Encounters of the third kind."

"Who said that?" Deborah moved quickly through the crowd, brandishing her microphone like a weapon. This could be the hottest scoop of her career, and she wanted to get the best quotes she could. She was positive her story would be picked up by the networks that night.

"Right here," a male voice said. Sarah was shocked to see it was Matt Neville.

"Now then," Deborah said, checking to make sure the camera crew was still with her. "What's this about UFO's?"

"It's all part of the time-space continuum," he said seriously. Matt looked completely sincere, his brown eyes fixed on hers, his expression solemn. Only Sarah knew that he was enjoying himself, spinning out the wildest story his imaginative brain could invent.

Deborah nodded, and glanced at her notes. Time-space continuum, she thought. Funny, she had never heard that expression. If there was such a thing, it would make great copy, though. If she could just figure out what this kid was talking about, she'd include it in her report.

"The way I see it," Matt said, "another Waterview High exists somewhere, identical to ours, in every detail. Every brick, every piece of chalk, every sweaty gym sock — each item in the school is copied exactly."

"Another Waterview High. . . ." Deborah was still smiling, but she looked a little suspicious. Her smile cracked a little at the part about the gym sock.

"Right. But this other Waterview High exists in a parallel universe, so we never encounter it." He paused for breath and then rushed on. "Of course, the theory of relativity can only explain so much, but if you consider the role of UFO's, it becomes apparent. . . ."

Deborah's smile was now permanently frozen in place. How could she get this kid to shut up? No one in the audience would have any idea what he was talking about, and the cameraman was giving her the "slashed-throat" signal, meaning it was time to cut. Thank goodness for a commercial, she thought gratefully.

"Thank you so much for joining us live, in this special telecast," she said to the camera.

Matt was still talking, but Deborah had regained possession of the mike and was walking rapidly away as the camera panned along. "We'll keep you updated, of course, and there will be film at six."

Film? Sarah thought. Film of what — a vacant lot? She and Aunt Pam were silent as a diaper commercial flashed across the screen. Sarah realized that Aunt Pam didn't have any instant answers for her, and suddenly she was eager to get back to her friends.

As if reading her thoughts, her aunt said, "I guess you know that we can't fix this overnight. I'll have to do some research, and maybe even make a few phone calls."

"I didn't think you'd be able to snap your fingers and make everything all right," Sarah said, wistfully. "I just wanted to make sure you were in on the problem from the start. Well, I guess I better get back to the schoolyard," she said standing up." She turned to her aunt. "Will I hear from you soon?"

Aunt Pam took both Sarah's hands in hers. "I'll call you the moment I've got any leads," she promised. Her eyes were golden, mysterious, warm with sympathy. "And try not to worry. I'm with you in this all the way."

* * *

It's impossible not to worry, Sarah thought, hurrying back to her friends. Aunt Pam had raised some disturbing questions. What if someone was trapped in the school building — a teacher perhaps, or maybe someone who worked in the office? Where were they now, what were they doing? They must be *very* upset, she thought guiltily. She concentrated as hard as she could, trying to come up with a mental picture of the school. Was it flying through space like the Little Prince? Was it caught in a time warp somewhere? Or maybe hovering around the planets, somewhere in outer space? *Anything* was possible. Waterview High could have landed in the next county, or it could be spinning around the sun. It had disappeared, that was the only thing she knew for sure. Just like she had wished, she added miserably.

She had just rounded the corner when she recognized Deborah Dodds approaching her. She was hurrying along, her high heels tapping on the pavement, while a cameraman scurried to keep up with her.

"I still think we need some better quotes," she was muttering. Her voice was annoyed, not bubbly and upbeat like the one she used on camera. "That last kid was a downer," she went on. "And all that garbage about time and space — he must have thought this was PBS!"

"He seemed bright enough," the cameraman said, shifting the heavy sound camera under his arm.

"Bright!" Deborah Dodd snorted. "Leave it to me to find the one teenaged Einstein in the bunch. Neville, he said his name was. You got him to sign a release form, didn't you?"

"Sure did," the cameraman said, tapping his pocket.

Sarah froze. They were talking about Matt.

"We'll go with it if we can't find anyone better," Deborah said flatly, "but as far as I'm concerned, the kid's dead wood. He sounds like he's from outer space himself. We could use just his voice, I suppose. Use the kid for a sound bite, while we run footage of the school. Or rather, the lot."

Dead wood? Sarah's temper flared. How could she talk about Matt that way! Deborah was almost up to her, when Sarah said coldly, "Matt Neville really is bright, you know. In fact, he's one of the smartest kids in our class."

Deborah stopped in her tracks. A funny look crossed her face, like she had stepped in something squishy, and then she gave a quick, professional smile. "So, you're one of Matt's classmates? And what is your name?" She whipped out a pad and pencil, motioning to her assistant to start filming.

"I . . . I'm Sarah Connell," Sarah said, wishing she had never opened her big mouth. She took a quick look at the camera and then stared at her feet. A red light was glowing, and there was a soft, whirring noise in the background. The darn thing is on! she thought. Sarah had never felt so uncomfortable in her life. She didn't want to be on television, but she couldn't think of any way of escaping Deborah Dodd. If she had been a more experienced witch, she probably could have come up with something on the spot, but it was impossible to think clearly with the reporter throwing questions at her.

"You're a little late, aren't you?"

"Late?" Sarah said nervously. What was she talking about?

Deborah made a big production out of staring at her watch. "It's almost nine-thirty. Everybody else has been at school for ages."

"Oh, that," Sarah said, suddenly understanding. "Well I was there earlier, but when I saw what had happened I — " She stopped, horrified. She had nearly said that she had gone to see her aunt who was a witch. Wouldn't that be great on the six o'clock news — Deborah Dodd would surely win an award for *that* scoop!

"You what?" Deborah was standing very close. She had a way of fixing her huge blue eyes on Sarah that made it hard to look away.

"I left to run an errand," Sarah said lamely.

Deborah permitted herself a brief, incredulous look, and then went on. "Everyone seems to have a theory about the school disappearing," she said smoothly. "What's yours?"

"I don't really have a theory," Sarah answered. She didn't know if she was supposed to look at Deborah or the camera, and finally picked a point over the reporter's left shoulder.

"Oh, come now," Deborah said pleasantly. "You must have *some* ideas. Everybody's entitled to one guess. We won't hold it against you." She chuckled, as if she and Sarah were sharing a private joke.

Sarah shook her head. "I have no idea what happened to the school, or why it disappeared."

"Well, do you think it will reappear?" Deborah interrupted her.

"Yes, I certainly hope so." The cameraman

stepped closer, and she wondered if her head was filling the screen, in one of those awful close-ups.

"When?" Deborah's voice was blunt, but Sarah refused to get rattled.

"Very soon, I would say. After all, it's only been gone for a couple of hours, so I'm sure that it will come back very quickly." She knew from the sudden gleam in Deborah's eyes that she had said something foolish — or even dangerous — but she had no idea what it was.

"Ah, I see," Deborah said, moving closer. Then she pounced for the kill. "That's very interesting, Sarah." She paused, giving a serious look to the folks at home. "And how do you know it's only been gone for a couple of hours?"

"Well, because it disappeared at 8:02," Sarah said. As soon as the words were out, she wanted to bite off her tongue. She knew it had disappeared at that time because she had glanced at the wall clock in the kitchen right before she made her "wish."

"That's fascinating," Deborah said. "And how did you come across that bit of information? How do you know it didn't disappear at seven-thirty, or six-thirty, or even late last night?"

Sarah felt her hands get clammy and she rubbed them against her jeans. "Well, I don't," she floundered. "I'm just guessing."

"Guessing?" Deborah arched her eyebrows. "And you just happened to pick a number like 8:02?" She shook her head, and her auburn pageboy fell back into place perfectly. "I'd say that was pretty bizarre, if you ask me," she said. She managed to look both concerned and thoughtful as she stared into the camera. "But this has been a pretty bizarre morning, here in Waterview, and we can only hope that things will soon be back to normal. I'm Deborah Dodds, for *Action News*." As soon as the red light went off, she turned to Sarah. "Look, I've got about a dozen more questions I want to ask you. Do you think — "

Sarah had no intention of sticking around for another interview. She had already made a terrible blunder, mentioning the time the school had disappeared, and her only desire now was to keep her mouth shut and blend into the crowd.

"Sorry," she said, running down the street. "I'm late for class."

"But there isn't any class!" Deborah yelled after her. She bit her lip in annoyance and turned to her cameraman. "Kids!"

Chapter 10

Sarah was relieved to see that Matt, Heather, and Micki were still standing right where she had left them. No one had seemed to notice her disappearance, and she casually rejoined the group, picking up the thread of the conversation.

"Did you really mean that stuff about spaceships?" Heather was saying to Matt. "I'd sort of hate to think of Waterview High landing on Mars, or something."

"There's not much chance of that," Matt said solemnly. "Mars is red-hot. If it landed there, it would be totally engulfed in flames."

"No kidding!"

"Anyway, you can relax," Matt said, chuckling. "I was just having a little fun with that reporter. She wanted to hear something sensational, so I figured I'd give it to her."

"You shouldn't have done that," Heather said reproachfully. "Everything you said might go out across the country tonight. The cameraman told me that we'll probably be on the network news." She couldn't help feeling excited at the thought. She knew it was really awful about the school disappearing, and a lot of people seemed upset about it, but still . . . a chance to be on national television!

Tina Jordan joined them a few minutes later, stamping her feet and pulling her cardigan tightly across her chest. "What's everybody still standing around for?" she muttered. "It's chilly."

"Nobody knows where to go," Sarah blurted out. It was true, she thought, glancing around the schoolyard. Kids were huddled everywhere in small groups, some were trying to look serious, others really were. The school administrators were clustered on the sidewalk with police officers, and their expressions were solemn. A few teachers were going from group to group, but they looked as confused as many of the kids did.

"There are so many unanswered questions," Micki said thoughtfully.

"You mean about what happened to the school?" Tina asked.

Micki shook her head. "No, that's a complete mystery. I mean, just from a practical viewpoint, what are we supposed to do now? We obviously aren't going to have school today, but no one's made any announcements."

"That's what I wondered," Tina said searchingly. "Are we supposed to stick around, or sign in?"

"I doubt they'd bother with sign-in sheets," Matt interrupted. "What would they do with them? The office is closed. I mean, gone."

They were all silent for a moment, and then Heather said suddenly, "Ohmigosh! Do you guys realize what this means? If the office is gone, all our records are gone." She grabbed Tina's sweater sleeve and started shaking it excitedly. "All our grades are gone! Remember that D I got in algebra — it's gone. Maybe forever!"

"But that's not good news," Micki said coolly. "If our grades are really gone, then how are we going to get credit for this year? I don't know about you, but I don't really feel like taking all our classes over again, so we can graduate."

"I hadn't thought of that," Heather said in a little voice.

Then Tina said, "There's no point hanging around in the rain to talk about it." She turned to her friends. "C'mon guys, we can grab a late breakfast at Carmichael's and figure out our next move."

A lot of the other kids must have gotten the same idea, Sarah realized, because Carmichael's was already jammed when they arrived a few minutes later. Heather managed to snare the last butcher-block table by the window, and everyone sat down quietly. The mood in the restaurant varied from high spirits to concern. There was some of the party atmosphere that usually accompanied school holidays, and some of the kids were just confused.

A small black-and-white TV was mounted on the wall, and Sarah was startled to see Deborah Dodds suddenly appear on the screen.

"Hush, everybody," Heather said, "she's talking about Waterview."

"There's good news and bad news in Waterview today," Deborah Dodds said brightly. She was wearing a trim blazer and sitting behind a high-tech desk in a television studio. To her right was a giant photograph of Waterview High School.

Why does she have to make a joke out of everything? Sarah thought. Deborah Dodds was beginning to get on her nerves. The woman would smile her way through a nuclear attack!

"The bad news, of course, is the fact that Waterview High has mysteriously disappeared." Deborah Dodds tried to look appropriately solemn, but Sarah knew that she was ready to burst into a toothy smile at any moment. "But here's the good news. We have it on good authority that no one was in the building at the time."

"Thank goodness for that," Sarah said feelingly. She was feeling guilty enough about making the school disappear — she didn't know what she would do if she were responsible for someone being injured or worse!

"And now, let's show you the footage we took earlier this morning at Waterview." A second later, Sarah jumped as she saw her own image flash on the screen.

"Sarah, you look great," Heather said. "If only it were in color."

"Shhh." Sarah silenced her by jabbing her hard in the arm. She sat frozen. What if they used that quote about the time? What would people think? A couple of minutes later, her hopes were dashed. Deborah used the entire interview, including the part where Sarah set the time of the disappearance at 8:02.

"That's funny," Heather said when they broke for a commercial.

Here it comes, Sarah thought. She tried to sound casual, but she noticed that Micki was giving her a speculative look out of the corner of her eye, and she wondered if she suspected the truth. "What's that?" Sarah asked, as casually as she could.

"Well, no offense, Sarah, but I just wondered why they used your interview instead of mine? Not that you weren't simply great on camera, but still. . . ."

Sarah relaxed as Heather gave a full account of her own interview with Deborah Dodds. She had total recall, it seemed, and by the time she had finished describing her big moment on camera, the cheeseburgers had arrived. Sarah was relieved when the conversation shifted to plans for the afternoon.

"There's no point in going back to school," Tina said, "so why don't we take in a movie?"

"You're on!" Matt agreed. "I'll even spring for the popcorn. How about you, Heather, are you coming with us?"

"Are you kidding?" Heather said incredulously. She delicately wiped her lips and picked up her check. "I'm getting home as fast as I can." She stood up, fluffing out her blonde hair. "I'm going to stay glued in front of the TV for the rest of the day. I just know that Deborah's going to use my interview, and I don't want to miss a single word!"

"Count me out, too," Sarah said, a moment later. "I need to get home . . . and straighten out some things."

"I'll walk you," Micki offered, giving her friend a quick smile. Sarah nodded, trying to read her expression and gave up. Was she just being nice, or did she suspect something?

A few minutes later, she had her answer. Micki knows, Sarah thought. She knows that somehow I'm involved in all this. She knows, but she's waiting for me to say something.

"I didn't realize you gave an interview," Micki said. They were walking down Front Street, and the sky was still overcast. "It was kind of a surprise, suddenly seeing you on TV, like that."

"I didn't get a chance to tell you," Sarah admitted, "but I went over to Aunt Pam's for a while while you were talking. I was on my way back to school when Deborah Dodds caught me." She shook her head, remembering how persistent the reporter had been. "Believe me, Micki, I didn't want to talk to her. There was just something about her. She has this way of making you say things you don't mean to."

"Aunt Pam's. Hmm, that's interesting. What were you doing over there?" Micki raised an inquisitive eyebrow. "What does she have to do with all this?"

"Nothing," Sarah said quickly. She paused. If she couldn't trust Micki, who could she trust? "Micki, I don't want you to have the wrong idea about Aunt Pam. She didn't make the school disappear. I did."

She glanced at Micki, but her expression hadn't changed, and she was still walking at the same pace. "Micki, did you hear me? I'm responsible for this whole mess. I made the school vanish!" She tugged at Micki's khaki trench coat, realizing she had seen one just like it in the window of Rugby's.

"I know," Micki said quietly. They were at a stop light, and she turned to face her friend. "And I knew you'd tell me when you were ready to."

"How did you know?"

Micki shrugged. "The look on your face, that funny little quiver you get in your voice when you're nervous. When you've known somebody for so long, you pick up on these things." She paused as the light changed, and they started across the street. "And of course, the television interview. That clinched it."

Sarah's spirits plummeted. Micki hadn't missed a thing. "The time?" she said grimly.

Micki's big brown eyes were serious. "I'm afraid it's quite a giveaway. How did you know the school disappeared at exactly 8:02, anyway?"

Sarah told her about Simon, the orange juice, and the kitchen clock. Micki listened carefully, and when she spoke, her tone was somber. "This isn't good, Sarah. It could cause real problems for you."

"Do you think so?" Sarah was worried. If Micki had picked up on her slip with Deborah Dodds, surely other people would pick up on it, too!

"Unless we can think of some perfectly reasonable explanation of how you knew it disappeared at that moment," Micki said slowly. "Unless, we say that you were standing in the schoolyard when it happened, and you glanced at your watch?"

"No good." Sarah shook her head. "My family knows I was late getting to school today.

Everybody was in the kitchen, and my mother even mentioned how late I was. I'm pretty sure she looked at the clock, too."

"Then that's out." She paused. "Does your Aunt Pam have any ideas?"

"She doesn't know what I said to Deborah Dodds. I could call her and tell her, but right now, she's trying to figure out a way of getting the school back. I don't want to distract her. She needs to focus all her energies on finding Waterview for us — the longer it's missing, the worse it will be." Sarah wondered what would happen if Waterview were *never* found, and pushed the thought away. There was no point in assuming the worst — Aunt Pam could work magic!

Micki thought for a moment. "I've got an idea. Now, this sounds a little far-out, but could you say that you had a premonition that the school would disappear, and that the number 8:02 just flashed into your head? I saw a psychic on TV, and he said things like that happened to him all the time."

"I saw him, too," Sarah said, making a face, "and he also said he was related to King Tut in another life." She turned up the collar on her red jacket. "I don't want to pretend I'm a psychic, Micki; people will think I'm a nut."

"Well, it's better than having them think you're a witch," Micki said reasonably.

"Not necessarily — " Sarah was walking a little ahead of Micki, and she stopped so abruptly, her friend tumbled into her.

"What's wrong?" Micki began, and then she saw it, too. "Oh, no," she whispered. "This is just what I was afraid of."

They were only a few yards away from Sarah's front porch, and if they hadn't been so wrapped up in their conversation, they would have noticed it before. It was certainly out of place in this quiet, tree-lined neighborhood, on this carefully tended street. It just didn't go with the neatly trimmed hedges and the solid stone houses. . . .

"Maybe it's a coincidence," Micki said.

"No," Sarah said. Her voice was barely a whisper. "It's no coincidence. It's here for me."

Micki searched her mind for something encouraging to say, and drew a blank. There was no doubt about it. The black-and-white police cruiser was waiting silently just a few feet away.

And it was parked right in front of Sarah's house.

Chapter 11

"Just stay cool," Micki ordered a couple of minutes later. "There's nothing to worry about." They stepped cautiously into Sarah's front hall, and Sarah's heart was pounding so loudly she was surprised Micki couldn't hear it. She tossed her jacket over the banister, trying not to make a sound, and froze when she heard voices coming from the kitchen.

"It's them!" She grabbed Micki's arm, as if to make a rush for the front porch, but Micki blocked her way.

"Calm down!" she hissed. "You're going to ruin everything."

"Sarah, is that you? Would you come out here for a minute, please? There are some people here to see you." Mrs. Connell's voice rang out from the kitchen. From somewhere upstairs,

Sarah heard the heavy beat of a Michael Jackson song. Simon and Nicole were safely up in their rooms, she thought.

"What's my mother doing home?" Sarah whispered. "Do you suppose they called her at work?"

"I don't know," Micki said, nudging her toward the kitchen. "But if you don't stop acting like a scared rabbit, this whole thing is going to blow up in your face."

"But — "

"No buts," Micki's voice was firm. "Just get in there and try to act natural. And remember, they can't prove anything."

Before she could object, Sarah found herself being propelled into the kitchen. She stopped in the doorway, taking in the scene at the kitchen table. Her mother was sitting drinking coffee with two uniformed police officers.

"Wow, just like *Dragnet*," Micki whispered.

"Sarah, this is Officer Clark and Officer Wendell," her mother said. "They have a few questions they'd like to ask you."

I'll just bet they do, Sarah thought. Like, what did you do with Waterview High?

"Fine," Sarah said. She had hoped her voice would sound strong and confident — and above all, innocent — but the word popped out in a frightened squeak. Micki gave her a sharp nudge, and together, they edged over to the table.

"This is her friend, Micki Davis," Mrs. Connell explained.

"Well, that's fine," Officer Clark said, half-raising from her chair. "Why don't you girls just sit down here, and we can get statements from both of you."

Statements! Sarah gave Micki a worried look. She knew about statements from *Hill Street Blues*. First you gave a statement, and the next thing you knew, you were handcuffed and whizzing your way down to the police station!

"Your name is Micki Davis?" Officer Wendell said. He whipped out a notebook, and asked Micki to spell her name, while Sarah sat in an agony of suspense. How many ways could there be to spell Davis? she thought irritably.

Officer Clark waited a moment and then said to Sarah, "Is there something you'd like to tell us about the disappearance of Waterview High?" Her voice was soft, and she looked at Sarah with friendly blue eyes. Everything about her said: "Trust me," but Sarah knew that was precisely the one thing she couldn't do!

She looked to Micki for advice, but Micki had ducked her head, and was staring at the paisley tablecloth as though she'd never seen it before. Sarah kicked her sharply under the table, and Micki shifted her gaze to the potted philodendron trailing over the counter. Sarah gave up. She was going to have to handle this on her own.

"What would I know about it?" she asked. She forced herself to look directly into those crinkly blue eyes, because she had read someplace that police officers notice things like that.

"I don't know," Officer Clark admitted. "I was hoping you could help us with this problem."

"I don't see how," Sarah said. She glanced at her mother, who was looking at her with a curious expression on her face. Had she seen the newscast? Sarah wondered.

"It's a total mystery," Micki said suddenly. "Everyone at school is really surprised, and nobody has the slightest idea what happened." Her voice seemed very loud in the quiet kitchen, and everyone looked at her with total absorption. Sarah saw Officer Wendell take out his notebook again, and scribble something in it.

"Really?" Officer Clark murmured.

"Really!" Micki said forcefully. She had picked up a paper napkin off the table, and was shredding it into a little pile. Officer Wendell was watching her every move, and Sarah figured he was probably trying to decide if he should make a note of it. "I just want you to know that Sarah and I have absolutely no idea what happened to Waterview High. No idea at all." She looked around the table, as if daring anyone to disagree with her.

"But that's not true," Officer Clark said. Her voice was deceptively gentle. "Sarah has some ideas." She paused dramatically. "She knows the school disappeared at exactly 8:02. I saw her say so on television." She exchanged a look with her partner. "Now, I wonder how she would know a thing like that?"

"I wondered the same thing," Mrs. Connell broke in. "How do you know that, Sarah?"

"I . . . I. . . ." Sarah felt herself wilting under Officer Clark's steady gaze. "That's hard to say," she finished weakly. No one spoke, and she realized they were obviously waiting for her to continue. "Deborah Dodds made me a little nervous," she began. "I meant to say that I figured the school had disappeared at eight o'clock . . . I heard all my friends say they got there *after* eight o'clock, and it was already gone." She put on her most sincere look, but Officer Clark's expression didn't change. Sarah wondered if the police officer believed her.

"But you said 8:02," Officer Clark said calmly.

"Oh, that!" Sarah paused, thinking fast. "That was just a slip of the tongue. You see, all the clocks at Waterview are set two minutes fast — I guess to keep the kids on their toes — so when it's really eight o'clock, the clocks say 8:02. Whenever I mean eight o'clock, I just automatically say 8:02."

"And that's all you know about it?"

"That's all I know about it." Sarah waited again.

Officer Clark decided to retreat. After a long, suspenseful moment, both officers rose together, as if on cue, and thanked everyone for their time. Sarah noticed that Officer Wendell asked Micki for her address as they walked down the hall.

"We'll be in touch," Officer Clark said. "If you think of anything. . . ." She let her voice trail off, and looked meaningfully at Sarah.

"We'll let you know," Sarah said firmly.

The moment they were out the door, Sarah let her breath out in a long sigh. She felt drained and exhausted. Her first police interrogation — no wonder!

Her mother was all set to start her own interrogation. Her eyes flickered from Sarah to Micki, and Sarah was sure that she suspected something. "Sarah — " her mother began, just as the phone rang. "Darn!" she said. "I'm expecting a call from work. Don't go away," she ordered. "I'll be right back."

For a moment, Micki and Sarah didn't speak. Then the silence was shattered by Simon thundering down the stairs, dragging Nicole with him. "Hey, that was great! I was waiting for them to pull out the handcuffs."

"You heard?" Sarah said wryly.

"Did we ever!" Nicole answered. "I liked the way you handled the cop," she said. "Don't call us, we'll call you," she giggled. "You should have seen Mom's face when the car pulled up. She thought you had been run over by a bus, or something."

"Yeah, it was really radical," Simon agreed. "She came back home because she'd forgotten her briefcase, and she found the house surrounded."

"Surrounded?" Sarah said, annoyed. Simon had a way of overdramatizing everything.

"Well, it's not every day you see a cop car parked outside your front door," he said defensively. "Say, Sarah," he began, "how did you know that — "

"I've got to go upstairs with Micki for a minute," Sarah broke in. "She wants to borrow something to wear tonight."

"Hey, wait a minute," Nicole objected. She stood in the middle of the stairs with her arms folded. "What are we supposed to say if reporters turn up? Plus, Mom wants to talk to you," she added, her blue eyes gleaming. She was always happy to see Sarah get in trouble, and she had the sneaking feeling that this was just the tip of the iceberg. Sarah could deny it all she wanted — but Nicole was *sure* that her sister knew something about Waterview disappearing!

"We'll be right down," Sarah yelled, heading up the stairs. "Five minutes, I promise."

"That was close, really close," Micki said. She made sure Sarah's bedroom door was tightly shut before collapsing on a throw cushion on the floor. "I think Nicole knows something," she said. "Or, I think she suspects that *you* know something."

"I don't care what she thinks," Sarah said,

falling on the bed. She tucked a pillow behind her head, and scrunched her feet under her. She always believed she did her best thinking in this position, and if ever there was a time for clear thought, it was right now. "The only thing that matters is those two cops."

"Officers Clark and Wendell," Micki said. "Do you think they were doing an act?"

"An act?"

"Well, I saw this movie once, and it said that cops always work in pairs. One comes on friendly, and one comes on tough, and that way, they break down your resistance."

"Micki, please!" Micki's imagination had a way of getting out of hand. "I've got more important things to worry about right now."

"You don't have to be so touchy," Micki said, and Sarah stared at her in surprise. She had just noticed something important: Micki wasn't acting quite so preppy. She still looked preppy and dressed preppy, but her voice was almost back to normal. Was the spell with Jonathan Brooks wearing off? If that was true, she'd probably wasted her time, starting that new spell with Jeff Tyson. . . . She forced her attention back to what Micki was saying. "I think you're in the clear for the time being, Sarah.

At least you managed to come up with an excuse for that 8:02 business. Very inventive," Micki said admiringly.

"I was desperate." A sudden thought hit Sarah. "Micki, what if they discover that I made up the whole thing — about the clocks being set fast, I mean."

"How could they?" Micki said mildly.

"They could check the — " Sarah stopped. No, that was silly. Of course they couldn't check the clocks. The school was gone, the clocks were gone. This whole thing was making her crazy!

"Look, I've got to run," Micki said, standing up.

"You're not leaving!" Sarah was aghast. "What if more reporters turn up? What if the police come back? What if somebody from school sees that interview and tips off the principal?"

"I think you'll be safe for a few hours," Micki told her. She buttoned up her trench coat, and ran a hand through her auburn hair. "And I really need to get right home. My mother's probably worried about me, and I wouldn't be surprised if that Officer Wendell decides to pay her a visit. If he does, I want to be there."

Sarah nodded. "You're right." She sighed. "I

just don't know how I'm going to handle all this stuff myself."

"You're not alone. You can call me the minute you hear anything, and I'll come right back. Plus, you probably should get in touch with Aunt Pam and see if she's made any progress."

"True," Sarah agreed. "I'll do that right now."

Micki gave her a quick hug. "Call me the second anything happens."

"Promise." Sarah smiled and gave her the thumbs-up sign. Micki quietly closed the door just as the phone started ringing. What now? She yanked it off the hook, expecting the worst.

"Sarah, I've been worried about you." It was David Shaw. His voice was warm and reassuring, and she grinned and dropped onto her bed. She cradled the receiver and pulled the quilt up around her knees.

"I just got home," she said. "Were you in the schoolyard this morning?"

"Yes, but I didn't see you, and I was afraid. . . ." He started laughing. "This sounds crazy, but I thought maybe you were missing or something. Along with the school."

"I'm fine," Sarah said. "You probably didn't see me, because I went over to Carmichael's with my friends."

"The whole thing is so amazing," he said. "I don't know what to make of it, do you?"

Thank goodness, Sarah thought. He must not have seen the interview with Deborah Dodds. "I haven't got a clue," she said.

"Well, I'm just glad that you're okay," he said. "I had kind of hoped we could get together today, but I have to work at the Pizza Palace."

"Today?"

"All day. And probably till late at night. My boss called to say that Waterview is going to be jammed with reporters and photographers, and they're all going to want pizza. The hotels are already booked up, so he'll probably do a fantastic business."

"People are coming to town for this?" Sarah said, horrified. She hadn't even thought of that possibility.

"You bet they are. *USA Today* and *60 Minutes* are already here, I've heard. And the *Today Show* will be here any minute. They chartered a plane out of New York — my boss told me all about it. After all, this is going to be the biggest news story of the year. Probably of the century! I've got to run, but I'll call you back as soon as I can. I really want to see you again."

"Me, too," Sarah said breathlessly. She hung

up a moment later, and closed her eyes. Things were going so perfectly with David, and she couldn't even take a moment to enjoy it. Wow, *60 Minutes*, the *Today Show*? Aunt Pam had to do something — fast.

Chapter 12

"Any news?" Sarah asked Aunt Pam twenty minutes later. She had run all the way to Plates and Pages, not even bothering to throw on a jacket, and she was shivering in her light cotton blouse.

"Not yet," Aunt Pam said soberly. She ushered Sarah up the winding wrought-iron staircase that led to her apartment. "But I've closed the shop for the day, so I can work without any interruptions."

"That's good," Sarah said fervently. "I'm afraid I can't stay long, because my mother will be looking for me." She quickly explained about the two police officers visiting the house. "Mom was still on the phone when I left, and I know she wants to talk to me."

"Well, sit down and relax, and I'll tell you what I've done so far. Look at you," she said, brushing Sarah's hair out of her eyes. "You're all out of breath."

"Don't worry about me," Sarah said. "I feel so terrible about what happened, I can't even think straight." She let Aunt Pam persuade her to sit in the big white lounging chair in front of the fireplace. It was so cozy that Sarah caught herself wishing she could just forget her troubles, close her eyes, and drift off to sleep.

She must have dozed for a few minutes, because she jumped when Aunt Pam suddenly appeared next to her. "Drink this," her aunt said, handing her a mug of orange tea. "And I'll bring you up-to-date." She adjusted a pair of horn-rimmed glasses on her nose, and flipped through a pile of computer printouts. She was wearing a deep purple warm-up suit, and had swept her thick black hair into a ponytail.

"Wherever Waterview High is," she began, "it's not in the continental United States." She peered owlishly at Sarah over her glasses. "I have sources checking out Hawaii and Alaska right this minute, and we should know something from Europe and the Far East tomorrow."

Sarah was impressed. "You mean witches use computers?" Sarah said, sitting straight up in her chair.

"We're way past the days of pointy hats and broomsticks," Aunt Pam said reprovingly. "I thought you knew that."

"Yes, of course," Sarah mumbled, "I just didn't realize how hi-tech you were."

"The point is, I can find out where Waterview High *isn't*, but not where it *is*."

"So what's the next step?"

"We have to find Waterview, and then figure out a way to transport it back here. The trouble is, it could be anywhere." Sarah felt a cold stab of fear. What if it never turns up? she wondered.

Her aunt must have noticed the bleak expression on Sarah's face, because she made an obvious effort to be cheerful. "Oh, don't worry. It's *somewhere*, of course," she went on. "It's not like it dropped into a black hole in space, and we can't recover it."

Sarah sipped her tea. One moment she was convinced that Waterview would reappear safely, and the next moment, she was afraid that it was lost forever. She knew that she wouldn't be able to focus on anything, not on

Micki and her romances, or David Shaw, until she knew that Waterview was back in place.

"Is there anything I can help you with?" Sarah asked. "Maybe some books I could check out, or some phone calls I could make?" She felt so helpless not being able to do anything!

"Not yet," Aunt Pam said. "I'm going to spend the next few hours going over those" — she pointed to a pile of clothbound books on her coffee table — "and see if there's anything from the past I can use."

"The past?"

"Previous spells, legends, old recipes. You can learn a lot from those books, Sarah, and when you're ready for some advanced training, I'll be glad to lend them to you. Some of them are almost a hundred years old, as you know," she said proudly.

Advanced training! Sarah thought. I've been making such a mess of things lately, I need a beginner course.

"The minute I can use your help, I'll call you," Aunt Pam said, walking her to the door. "But right now, I think you'd better hurry home. Your mother wants to see you."

"You have a premonition?" Sarah asked curiously. She wondered if Aunt Pam suddenly pictured her mother pacing up and down the kitchen floor, wringing her hands, and looking annoyed.

"Of course not," her aunt laughed. She wrapped a thick wool poncho around Sarah's shoulders. "She called while you were napping before. I said I'd send you home as soon as you finished your tea."

"Oh," Sarah said, relieved. She ran home, and the wind didn't even bother her this time. Maybe it was the warm Peruvian poncho that she clutched tightly around her, or maybe it was just that Aunt Pam had a way of lifting her spirits. Whatever the reason, Sarah felt much better than she had an hour earlier. Just as well, she thought. Because now I have to face the family. . . .

Everyone was in the kitchen when Sarah got home, and her father was deep in conversation with her mother. He had spent the whole day taking care of patients, she realized, and now her mother was probably filling him in about Waterview. And about the police visit, she thought. Her father spotted her just then, and she wondered if she could safely duck upstairs to her room.

Too late. "What's this I hear about my

daughter being a celebrity?" His voice was hearty, but his expression was serious. "Some of my patients said they saw you on television."

"Oh, nothing, Dad," she said lightly. "A lot of the kids were being interviewed, and I . . . was just one of them." She opened the refrigerator and started pulling out vegetables. "Hey, how about if I make one of those giant tossed salads you like — I'll even add sprouts."

She was reaching for the cutting board, when her father stopped her. "I heard it was a pretty unusual interview. At least, the police seemed to think so." He was looking very intently at her, and Sarah wondered exactly how much she should say. She noticed Nicole and Simon huddled over a plate of brownies, pretending to be reading magazines, but listening to every word.

"They . . . uh . . . made a big deal out of some little thing I said, that's all," Sarah explained. She glanced at her mother for support, but Mrs. Connell was standing with her arms folded, waiting to hear more.

"Some little thing," Simon muttered with a mouthful of chocolate. "They wanted to know how Sarah knew exactly the time the school disappeared."

"You knew the time it happened?" Her father looked grim.

"To the second," Simon answered for her.

"That's impossible," Sarah blurted out. "They can't prove that. No one knows for sure what time it . . . left."

"Oh, yes, they do," Nicole piped up. "If you had stuck around instead of running over to Aunt Pam's, you would have seen the latest news update. Mr. Ferris said just what you said — that it disappeared at 8:02."

"How would he know that?" Sarah said weakly.

"It's simple." Nicole smiled, pleased with herself. "He was heading up the front steps at exactly eight o'clock, then he remembered he left some test papers in his car, so he walked back to the parking lot. He got the papers off the front seat, turned around, and the school was gone."

"They had him retrace his steps," Simon said eagerly. "And it took exactly two minutes to go through all the motions." He then downed a glass of milk and looked at Sarah admiringly. "Hey, are you a psychic, or something? That would be cool!"

"Of course not!" Sarah said irritably. "I don't know anything about it. I've already talked to the police, I don't know why I have to be interrogated by my own family."

Her father hurried over to her and put his arm around her. "We didn't mean to interrogate you, Sarah. We're just curious about how you happened to pick the right time."

"It was just a coincidence," her mother said. At last, Sarah thought gratefully. There was a long moment when no one said anything. "Well," Mrs. Connell said brightly, "what do you say we have dinner in the den and watch the evening news? I've got the feeling that we won't want to miss a word of it tonight."

Sarah hurried upstairs the minute dinner was over. The school disappearance was the lead story on the national news, and her interview with Deborah Dodds had been picked up by all three networks. Sarah realized with a sinking feeling that this was just the beginning. Until the reporters had another lead, she would be featured over and over again. After all, how many times could you watch the principal and the police chief say they had absolutely no idea what happened? The reporters were desperate for a story, any story, and Sarah knew that once her name got out, they wouldn't leave her alone.

She thought about calling Aunt Pam, but decided not to interrupt her. She knew her aunt would contact her the minute she knew something, and anyway, she could spend the whole day with her tomorrow. Since there was no school, she obviously would have plenty of free time.

Sarah flopped onto her bed, looping her arm around Bandit, who was sleeping on the pillow. She'd rest for a few minutes, she decided, and then plan her strategy.

The next thing she knew, her mother was shaking her awake. "Micki's here," Mrs. Connell said. "She wants to see you."

"Micki?" Sarah realized with a start that she had fallen asleep in her clothes. "What time is it?"

"Nearly eight." Her mother opened the drapes a little, and harsh sunlight flooded the room. "In the morning." She smiled sympathetically. "You must have been wiped out. You slept right through the night like that."

"Gosh, I can't believe it." Then she noticed that her mother was wearing a sweater and jeans. "You're not going into work today?"

"I can't." She motioned to the window. "Take a look outside, and you'll see what I mean. But stand back out of sight."

Sarah stumbled to the window and saw a

navy blue van parked across the street. "Police?"

"Worse," her mother said ruefully. "Reporters and photographers. They've been knocking at the door since six, asking for an interview. I'm surprised you slept through all the noise."

"So am I," Sarah said. She took a look in the mirror and flinched. Wild hair, rumpled clothes, shiny face. She looked a mess. "Tell Micki I'll be out in five minutes," she said, heading for the shower.

She appeared at the breakfast table in six minutes flat, with wet hair. It didn't matter what she looked like, because Micki was so excited, she could hardly talk.

"Sarah, you're not going to believe this!" Micki was wearing a black warm-up suit with suede boots. Sarah had the vague idea that something was wrong, but her brain was too full to deal with it.

"Try me," Sarah said.

"Look! It's you!" Micki said triumphantly. "You're famous!" She thrust a tabloid paper under Sarah's nose, and tapped it with her fingernail. "Right here!"

Sarah tried to focus on the tabloid in front of her. It was the same paper she always read in the checkout lane at the supermarket, and her eyes skimmed the crazy headlines. "Eighty-year-old woman trains a duck to talk?" she said, puzzled. "Chimpanzee discovers cure for arthritis?"

"No, *here*," Micki said impatiently. She snatched the paper away and began to read: "Waterview cheerleader linked to school disappearance."

"What?" Sarah grabbed the paper away from Micki, just as Mrs. Connell joined them. "I don't believe this," she muttered. "Where do they get this stuff? They've got it all wrong. In the first place, I'm not a cheerleader — "

"They made a lot of other mistakes. They also say you're blonde and cute," Micki pointed out, smiling.

"Thanks a lot," Sarah said sarcastically.

Mrs. Connell said, sitting down, "I want to see what they wrote." She read the first paragraph, shaking her head in disgust. "In an exclusive interview today — ha!" She read silently, frowning.

"How bad is it?" Sarah asked. Suddenly another worry hit her. Aunt Pam! "Mom," she said quickly, "do they mention the rest of the family?"

Her mother nodded. "Yes, but they've got us all mixed up. They say that Simon is away in college and that Dad is a chiropodist. I'm listed as a teacher . . . well, that's probably close enough. Oh, no!" she put her hand to her mouth, and started laughing. "They say that we have four cats, a collie, and a Shetland pony."

"What's so funny about that?" Micki asked.

"They think Nicole is the collie."

"Very funny," Nicole snapped, walking into the kitchen. "Simon just woke me up to say that something weird was going on down here." She glared at Sarah. "Well, you weren't satisfied until you got us in the newspaper, were you?"

"Nicole!" Mrs. Connell said sharply. "Sarah didn't give these people any interviews. She's just as upset by all this as you are."

More, Sarah longed to say. After all, she had more to worry about than bad publicity. She had to help Aunt Pam figure out a way to get the school back. And she had to do it today!

She managed to escape upstairs to her room with Micki after everyone ate breakfast. "That was a really crummy thing those reporters did," Micki said. "Do you think your parents are upset?"

"They're not thrilled over it," Sarah said. She sat down at her dressing table and started to comb out her curly brown hair. "What really worries me is what's going to happen next. Once people see that article, they'll be camping outside."

"They didn't really say you knew anything," Micki pointed out. "They just said you were being questioned."

"I know, but it's what they hinted at. People will expect the worst, they always do." She stared at Micki. She really did seem different, not preppy at all anymore. She was wearing a jaunty warm-up suit, and her hair was brushed back.

"I guess you'll have to stick close to home today, won't you?" Micki asked. "I don't know if you noticed that blue van parked across the street."

"I did," Sarah assured her. "And I bet they're going to pounce on me the minute I set foot outside the front door."

"Afraid so. They tried to get me to talk when they saw me ringing the bell."

Sarah put down her comb and stared at her friend in astonishment. "Really? What did you say?"

"I said I was collecting for new band uniforms and asked them if they'd like to make a contribution."

"Good thinking!"

"Well, I knew it was the only way I could get in here without a hassle. . . ."

Sarah tuned out the rest of what Micki was saying and stared at herself in the mirror. There *had* to be a way of getting out of the house without being noticed by the reporters. She couldn't stay cooped up inside all day — she had work to do! She looked at Micki's coppery hair and had an idea. The reporters were expecting a blonde, or maybe a brunette . . . so why not be a redhead? It was risky, it was crazy, but it just might work!

"Micki," she began. "I need your help. . . ."

Chapter 13

Ten minutes later, a transformed Sarah stared at herself in the mirror. "What do you think?" she said eagerly.

"Not bad, not bad at all." Micki walked around her slowly. "I'm surprised you can fit into my boots."

"They're killing me," Sarah admitted. "But it's a small price to pay, if it helps me get past those reporters." She had switched clothes with Micki, grateful that she could wriggle into her friend's one-size-fits-all warm-up suit without any trouble. Funny, she thought, zipping up the velour jacket, Micki never wears sporty clothes like this.

Sarah's long hair was a bigger problem, but by pinning it up and using a can of auburn spray tint her chestnut hair was now a red color. It wouldn't fool anyone up close, she realized, but she hoped that if she walked fast, and ducked her head, no one would give her a second glance.

"Wish me luck," she whispered, as they tiptoed down the hall. When they were at the bottom of the steps, Micki, dressed in Sarah's clothes, opened the front door for her.

"Thanks again," Sarah called loudly. "Be sure to come to our band concert." She saw the driver of the van look up inquisitively. She trotted down the steps, and pretended to check off another address on a list. Just as she suspected, the man in the van yawned and turned back to his partner. Trembling with excitement, she forced herself to walk slowly to the corner, where she broke into a run.

"I did it!" she murmured. "I got away from them!"

It was a beautiful, sunny morning in Waterview, and Sarah wondered how her friends were going to spend the day. No one knew when school would start again — the principal had cancelled all classes, until he could find a place to hold them.

She avoided the main streets, just in case some nosy reporters might recognize her from the picture, and took the back way to Aunt

Pam's. As she suspected, the CLOSED sign was still in the window of Plates and Pages, but her aunt spotted her from her upstairs apartment. "I'll be right down," she yelled. A moment later, Aunt Pam opened the door, and swept her into an enthusiastic hug. "I think we've got something," she said. Her lovely golden eyes were shining with excitement, and her black hair tumbled down her back in a mass of waves.

"You think you found the school?" Sarah said, as her aunt nudged her toward the winding staircase.

"I've got a couple of very good leads," Aunt Pam told her. She pointed to a stack of books on the floor. She waved her hand and half a dozen silver bracelets clattered together. "I started by looking up everything I could find under wishes, spells, and disappearances, and then I went on to lost buildings and cities."

For the next half hour, Aunt Pam went over her strategy with Sarah. She opened an ancient book that was filled with strange symbols written on parchment, and explained their significance to Sarah. "I've tried to be logical about this," she said, consulting a yellow legal pad on the coffee table, "and I decided to start by dividing the galaxy into quadrants."

"Quadrants?" Sarah had no idea what she

was talking about, except that it reminded her of geometry class.

"Fourths," Aunt Pam said briefly. "I know that three is supposed to be the magic number," she added apologetically, "but I've found that working in fourths really narrows the field."

"Narrows the field," Sarah murmured.

"So you see," Aunt Pam said, "when you compute the longitude and latitude, in terms of the vernal equinox, you see that there's a good chance Waterview is right here." She stabbed the map with a long, beautifully polished fingernail.

Sarah looked down and gasped in surprise. "Waterview High is in the middle of the Indian Ocean?" She didn't know what she was expecting, but she was stunned by the news.

"Unless I forgot to figure in the time difference at the equator," Aunt Pam said thoughtfully. "And that's assuming that the eclipse a couple of years ago didn't throw off my calculations."

"But, I don't understand," Sarah said. "If it's in the ocean, is it. . . ." She paused, trying to visualize the school lying on the ocean floor. It's probably soggy and covered with barnacles, she thought.

"It's not necessarily *in* the ocean," Aunt Pam pointed out. "It's *at* this point. In other words, it's somewhere above or below the ocean, at these particular coordinates."

"Above the ocean? How could that be?"

Aunt Pam shrugged. "It could very well be high above the ocean — occupying the air space, you see."

Sarah shook her head in amazement. It was even harder to imagine Waterview High floating in space! "Wow," she said softly. "So what's the next step?"

"That's where you come in," Aunt Pam said. Her voice was steady, and she had a determined look on her face. "We'll have to bring it back, and we better do it tonight, or it might stay there for another hundred years."

"Tonight," Sarah breathed. It sounded exciting, and also a little scary. What if they couldn't bring it back? "What time?"

Aunt Pam punched a few buttons on her calculator and raised her eyebrows. "Just as I thought. The planets will be in the right alignment exactly at midnight, so that's when we need to cast the spell."

"Midnight?"

Her aunt nodded and took her hand. "There's no other way, Sarah. If we don't get it back tonight. . . ." She shrugged, and her voice trailed off. "Can I count on you? You'll have to meet me here and we'll walk over there together."

"I'll do it," Sarah said firmly. She was definitely not thrilled at the idea of going to the schoolyard at midnight with Aunt Pam, but what could she do? She was the one who had started this whole mess!

"Oh, and Sarah, there's one more thing."

"Yes?" Sarah was standing up and zipping up her jacket.

"I don't want to hurt your feelings, but I'm not sure red is your color."

"My color?" Sarah drew a blank, and then started laughing. She had forgotten to explain to Aunt Pam about her tinted hair. "Don't worry, Aunt Pam, it will be gone by tonight."

Sarah felt too keyed up after her meeting with Aunt Pam to go home, so she decided to pay a quick call on Micki. They were settled in Micki's room with apple juice and peanut butter sandwiches when Sarah first suspected that something was different. It began when they traded clothes again. Micki had slipped back into her warm-up suit, and then, surprisingly, had wrapped a bright yellow sweatband across her forehead. It went very well with the outfit, Sarah thought, but Micki was such a "shetland sweater and knee socks" sort of person, that it came as a shock. And Mickie was wearing running shoes, Sarah noticed. New, expensive ones, just like the jocks wore. "Nice shoes," she couldn't resist saying.

"I just got this sudden urge to go jogging this afternoon," Micki told her. Sarah watched while Micki fastened a pair of weights around each wrist. It looked like she was wearing terry-cloth handcuffs.

"And you're going to wear those?" Sarah asked, pointing to the weights.

Micki shrugged. "If you're going to jog, you might as well get the maximum benefit out of it. You know what they say, 'no pain, no gain.' "

No pain, no gain? Micki the preppy had vanished, Sarah was happy to see, but this new Micki was a little unsettling. If she didn't know better, she would say that Micki was turning into a jock.

"Guess who called and asked me out?" Micki said coyly.

Sarah took a deep breath. She knew what was coming. "Haven't got a clue," she said, and hoped she sounded sincere.

"Jeff Tyson!" Micki was grinning from ear to

ear. "I knew you'd be surprised. We're going out this Saturday afternoon. There's a hockey game he wants to see."

"I didn't know you were into hockey," Sarah said, amused. She was right — a completely new side of Micki was emerging. What had happened to Jonathan? she wondered. Had the spell worn off, all by itself?

"Well, I didn't used to be," Micki hedged "but Jeff is such a big fan, that I'm trying to like it." She paused. "He's really cute, isn't he?"

"He sure is," Sarah said automatically. She took a bite of her sandwich and nearly gagged when a warning bell went off in her brain.

"I was really surprised because I never thought he liked me. Anyway," Micki went on cheerfully, "it was really kind of weird, because Jeff just called up to say he had this urge to see me . . . can you imagine such a thing?"

"I can imagine." Sarah watched as Micki started doing a series of deep-knee bends. She tried not to let the shock she felt register on her face.

"We started talking, and a funny thing happened." She stopped exercising long enough to look at Sarah. "I realized that I have always been attracted to him!"

"I . . . I hope the evening goes well," Sarah

managed to say. She felt queasy inside — had she really been able to start a romance between Micki and Waterview's biggest jock with just a *phone* call?

"Oh, I'm sure it will," Micki said. "Jeff said he wants to see a lot of me, so I guess this could be the start of something really big."

"Good, you're here in plenty of time," Aunt Pam said that night. She handed Sarah a flashlight as she locked the door to Plates and Pages.

"I've been waiting all day for this," Sarah said seriously. "If this doesn't work, Aunt Pam. . . ." She felt a lump of apprehension rise in her throat. What if her aunt's spell fell flat, and Waterview High stayed trapped somewhere in the Indian Ocean forever? It would be absolutely, one-hundred-percent her fault, and she knew she'd feel awful about it for the rest of her life!

"Sarah, let's give it a chance, before we start expecting the worst." Aunt Pam's voice was warm and encouraging, but Sarah wondered if her aunt had the same doubts that she did. Her aunt had done a lot of remarkable things with her powers, but this was the first time she was attempting something on this scale.

They walked briskly to the schoolyard, and

were relieved to see that there were no reporters or photographers in sight. There
wasn't even a security guard posted on the
property, because as Aunt Pam had said, there
was nothing left to guard!

"Good, we have the place all to ourselves,"
Aunt Pam said. She glanced at her watch and
spread a plaid blanket on the dirt. "You might
as well sit down, we have to wait for eight more
minutes."

Sarah sat down nervously and glanced at the
sky. There was a full moon and the silvery light
cast eerie shadows over everything. She had a
funny, quivery feeling in the pit of her stomach,
and she knew that if Aunt Pam hadn't been
with her, she would have been scared out of
her wits.

She noticed that Aunt Pam was remarkably
calm. She had brought a small book with her,
and had both hands folded over an open page.
"Is . . . that the spell?" she asked timidly.

Aunt Pam nodded. "You can see it if you
like." She passed the book to Sarah, but it was
written in a strange language she had never
seen before, and after a moment, she gave it
back. "Someday I'll teach you how to read it,"
her aunt promised.

"Don't worry about that. Just concentrate on

tonight," Sarah pleaded. If this works, she thought, I'll never ask for anything again.

Before Sarah had the chance to say another word, Aunt Pam rose, gathering her black wool shawl around her. She stood very still in the moonlight and began reciting words from the book. Her voice was clear and musical, and Sarah listened, fascinated. After a few moments, Aunt Pam stopped.

Then they waited. Dead silence, while Sarah silently ticked off the seconds in her head. How long would it take, she wondered. Suddenly she heard a loud rumbling in the sky — like an express train going at top speed — and a building came crashing down next to them!

"You did it!" Sarah scrambled to her feet and hugged her aunt. "Oh, thank goodness it worked. I was so afraid. . . ." She buried her face against her aunt's shoulder, and was surprised when Aunt Pam gently pushed her away.

"Don't congratulate me yet, Sarah," she said sadly. "I'm afraid we have a bit of a problem."

"A problem?" Sarah pulled away from her aunt and peered into the darkness. Then she saw the outlines of the turrets, the rugged gray stones, the tiny slit windows, and something that looked like a circular swimming pool. "A moat?" she whispered. "Aunt Pam, there's a moat!" she cried. "This isn't Waterview, this is a. . . ."

"Scottish castle," Aunt Pam said with a sigh. "Oh, darn, just when things were going so well."

"A Scottish castle?" Sarah kneeled on the blanket, dazed.

"Well, we better get rid of it quickly before it settles too long," her aunt said briskly. She snapped her fingers, and with a giant gust of wind, the castle vanished. "There," she said cheerfully, "it probably wasn't gone long enough for anyone to notice."

"Aunt Pam. . . ."

"Now, don't worry, Sarah. I'll get it right this time." She thumbed through the book, and tried again. This time the words had a lilting sound to them. They didn't have long to wait, because as soon as Aunt Pam had finished, there was a great crack of thunder. Aunt Pam smiled. "This is it!" she said, joining Sarah on the blanket. "Put your fingers in your ears, it's going to be noisy."

There was a loud ringing noise and then a loud crash as something heavy plummeted to earth. Something like a building? Sarah wondered. A curtain of dust rose in the their faces, and it was impossible to see. They stood up as the dust slowly settled, and the outlines of a familiar brick building took form.

Waterview High was back.

Chapter 14

The next day was one of the most confusing that Sarah had ever spent, and also one of the happiest. Part of Aunt Pam's spell had involved "selective amnesia," and she had arranged it so that no one, except Micki, would have any memory of Waterview High's disappearance. Sarah found it hard to imagine, but according to Aunt Pam, no one would ever mention the event again, or remember it in any way. It would be just as if the whole thing had never happened! Newspaper clippings — including the article about Sarah — would be erased, and television and radio tapes would be hopelessly scrambled. Things would be completely back to normal.

When Sarah's alarm went off at six that

morning, her first feeling was one of relief. It's over! she thought happily. It had been very late when she had gotten back from the schoolyard, and she had stayed awake for a long time, too excited to sleep. In her mind, she replayed the midnight scene with Aunt Pam over and over again. When Waterview had finally appeared in a cloud of dust, she thought it was the most beautiful sight she had ever seen.

She tumbled out of bed and reached for her robe, feeling tired and happy. The school was back, no one was hurt, and now she could get on with her life. She passed Nicole on the way to the shower, and for a moment, she was startled at her sister's casual greeting. Then she reminded herself that strange as it seemed, Nicole had no memory of all the turmoil and excitement of the past few days — to her, this was just another morning.

Sarah stayed in the shower a long time, letting the hot water play over her neck and shoulders, while she thought about Micki. Sarah felt funny about "engineering" Micki's social life.

"Pinch me, I'm dreaming," Tina said a few hours later. "They *couldn't* have done it again!" She nudged Sarah in the elbow as they inched their way through the cafeteria lunch line.

"What's that?" Sarah asked. She looked happily around the crowded lunchroom. Everything looked wonderful to her: the pale tile walls, the sickly green linoleum floor, and most of all, the horde of noisy students. Someone dropped a whole pile of empty trays next to her, and she didn't even flinch. She knew that nothing could spoil her great mood today. It's so terrific to have everything back in place, she thought. She felt very grateful that Aunt Pam had managed to pull off the biggest success of her whole career.

Tina jabbed her finger in the air. "That!" she said disgustedly. "How could they have come up with it twice in one week?"

Sarah followed her gaze and burst out laughing. There, on the menu board were the dreaded words: LUNCH SPECIAL: TASTY MEAT LOAF. "Oh, that," Sarah said, wiping her eyes. "It's pretty funny, isn't it?"

"Pretty funny, is that all you can say, *pretty funny*?" Tina slammed a carton of chocolate milk on her tray. "Well, I don't think it's one bit funny." When she saw she wasn't getting anywhere with Sarah, she turned to Matt. "What do you think, Matt? It seems impossible that it turned up again, doesn't it?"

"Not really," Matt replied calmly. "Statistically, it's not uncommon for a random event to occur twice in one week."

"Oh, no," Micki offered, reaching for a dish of macaroni and cheese. "Now you've gotten him started." Sarah stared at her friend in surprise. Micki *hated* macaroni and cheese.

"And 'Tasty Meat Loaf' isn't exactly a random event," he said thoughtfully. "I've noticed it seems to occur the day after they serve 'tasty hamburgers.' "

Everyone moved quickly past the Tasty Meat Loaf. Sarah watched as Micki carefully chose her lunch: a tossed green salad, a whole wheat roll, and a dish of unsweetened applesauce. She's eating like she's in training, Sarah thought idly. And then she realized that Micki *was* in training — she was in training for jock-of-the-year, Jeff Tyson!

As soon as they were seated, Micki whipped out a magazine and began to read. Sarah was surprised. None of her friends read at lunchtime.

"Who's on the cover of *Seventeen* this month?" Tina asked.

Micki looked up briefly and showed them the

cover. "It's not *Seventeen*, it's *Sports Illustrated*." She went right back to her article, her auburn head bent over the magazine.

Tina flashed a bewildered look at Sarah. "Uh, Micki," she began, "when did you start reading a magazine like that?"

Heather Larson chuckled. "When she learned it was full of cute guys," she said.

"I don't read it for the cute guys," Micki said coolly. "I read it to keep up with sports celebrities. They did a feature on one of my favorites this month." She tapped a glossy picture with her finger, and everyone stopped eating to look. "One of the all-time greats," she said firmly.

"Whatever you say," Heather said with a shrug. She turned and whispered to Sarah, "I don't recognize him, do you?"

Sarah squinted for another look, then shook her head. Micki's "favorite" was a beefy-looking guy dressed in a football uniform with enormous shoulder pads. As far as Sarah could see, he looked like every football player she had ever seen.

As if on cue, a husky voice broke into her thoughts.

"I thought I'd find you here, Micki." It was

Jeff Tyson, and Micki swiveled around in her chair to smile at him. Her whole face lit up, just like it had for Jonathan, and she patted the empty chair next to her. He wasn't bad-looking, Sarah thought, with his friendly grin and his crinkly blue eyes. In fact, he looked a lot like the celebrity on the magazine cover.

"Can you sit down for a minute?"

"Just for a second. I'm late for basketball practice."

"You mean you have to practice at lunch-time?" Heather said, surprised.

"It's not required," Jeff admitted. "But I told the coach I'd go down to the gym and work on my hook shots."

"Maybe we can see each other after school?" It was impossible to ignore the wistful note in Micki's voice.

"I don't think so," Jeff said briskly. "I've got to put in some extra time in the weight room. My deltoids could use some toning, and I think I may go for a little more definition in the bi-ceps. What do you think?" He flexed his upper arm. Micki watched, totally absorbed.

"Great definition," she said approvingly.

He flexed his arm a few more times. "Yeah, I guess you're right," he said, satisfied. "Like the coach always says, you can't improve on perfection." Sarah waited for him to laugh, but he didn't. Ohmigosh, she thought. This is scary. He really means it!

Tina Jordan, who had been eavesdropping shamelessly, rolled her eyes. She exchanged a long look with Sarah, and her meaning was clear: Why is Micki wasting her time with this jock jerk?

Jeff stood up then, and chucked Micki affectionately under the chin. "See ya tonight," he promised. "We'll catch the early show at the Strand."

The minute he was gone, Tina spoke up. "Micki," she said in a puzzled tone, "since when did you start dating jocks?"

Micki's brown eyes flashed as she put down her fork. "Jeff Tyson is not a jock," she said coldly.

"Really?" Heather giggled. "You could have fooled me."

"Then what is he?" Tina prodded her.

Micki took a long swallow of milk. "Jeff is one of the most talented, sensitive boys I have ever met."

"Even if his IQ is the same as his resting pulse," Matt murmured from the end of the table. Sarah shot him a warning glance.

"Tell me about your date tonight," Sarah said encouragingly. "What's on at the Strand?"

"The new Chuck Norris movie," Micki answered brightly. "Jeff's working on his brown belt in karate, and he wants to check out some of the moves."

"It sounds . . . uh, fascinating," Sarah said doubtfully. Her stomach felt like someone had dropped a cold stone in it. The new jock-Micki was even worse than the preppy-Micki. She never should have started this!

"It was a toss-up," Micki said regretfully. "The wrestling championships are on TV tonight, and it was a real temptation to stay home. But Jeff finally decided that it would be better if we taped them, and then we could watch them together on Friday."

"How romantic," Tina whispered.

"Then on Saturday there's the big game between the Atlanta Hawks and the Dallas Mavericks. We're going to watch that at my house," Micki said proudly.

"I didn't even know you liked baseball," Sarah said plaintively. The new Micki was a complete mystery to her, and she didn't like being shut out of her life.

"They're basketball teams," Micki said reproachfully. "Pro leagues. I'm surprised you didn't know that."

"That's what you get for not watching the *Wide World of Sports*," Matt teased.

"You're absolutely right," Micki said.

"It sounds like you've got a big weekend planned," Tina said wryly. "You and Jeff must have really hit it off."

"Oh, we have," Micki insisted. "You can't imagine how much we have in common."

"No, I wouldn't," Sarah muttered.

"In fact, I don't know how we're going to cram it all in," Micki said happily. "There's the *AC Delco Classic* on Saturday afternoon — that's the biggest bowling event of the year," she added for Sarah's benefit.

"It sounds like a laugh a minute," Tina observed.

"And Jeff's favorite fishing show is on at seven-thirty; he never misses it." She paused. "They're visiting a trout farm this weekend."

"Fascinating," Tina murmured. "Anybody for dessert?" she said, changing the subject. "Who wants to split a piece of chocolate cake with me?"

"Not me," Micki said, patting her flat stomach. "I don't eat white sugar or white bread anymore. Jeff says that if I want to build muscle, I should stick to complex carbohydrates."

So that explains the macaroni and cheese, Sarah thought. She bounced out of her chair the moment the bell rang, eager to escape the lunchroom. There was no doubt about it. She had made a gigantic mistake in casting that spell on Jeff Tyson. Wrestling matches, fishing shows, televised bowling — she'd never get to see Micki anymore!

"She's driving me crazy," Sarah said to Aunt Pam later that afternoon. "All she talks about are biceps and triceps, and I can't take it any longer!"

Aunt Pam smiled sympathetically. They were sitting in her spacious apartment, and the late afternoon sun seemed to be setting right over her aunt's balcony. "I suppose you think you've created a monster," she suggested.

"You bet I have!" Sarah said feelingly. "Micki spent a whole half hour talking about lactose build-up today. Lactose build-up! If I wanted to hear about that, I would have had lunch with my chemistry teacher."

"What was it like being back at school?" her aunt asked. She leaned forward, her chin resting in her hand. "Did anything seem different, or strange?"

"No, not at all," Sarah told her. She stirred her orange tea with a cinnamon stick and said thoughtfully, "It was wonderful. It's funny, but I never really appreciated Waterview before. It took a disaster before I realized how much I really like the place. Does that make sense?" she asked.

Aunt Pam nodded solemnly. "It makes a lot of sense. But I hope you don't decide to make anything else disappear. It was touch and go there for a while, you know."

"Oh, don't worry," Sarah said, laughing. "I've learned my lesson. From now on, I'll be very careful what I wish for."

They were silent for a moment, watching the setting sun.

"The selective amnesia worked, didn't it?" Aunt Pam asked. "It's the first time I've tried anything like that on such a big scale."

"It worked perfectly. Everything is right back the way it was, and nobody except Micki has a clue that the school was gone for a couple of days. And I trust Micki." Sarah looked glum.

"Of course, Micki is so hooked on this boy called Jeff Tyson right now, that I doubt anything would shake her up. And I have only myself to blame!" She explained about the spell she had cast, while her aunt listened carefully. When she finished, Sarah stared glumly into her teacup. "I hate to ask you for another favor, but you don't suppose you could. . . ." She gave Aunt Pam her most appealing smile.

"You want me to snap my fingers and undo the spell you put on Jeff?"

"Is that too much to ask?" Sarah said worriedly. "I know you advised me against doing it in the first place."

Aunt Pam looked directly into her eyes. "If I do, will you promise to leave Micki alone, and let her find her own boyfriend in her own good time?"

"Yes, I promise — " Before the words were out of Sarah's mouth, Aunt Pam snapped her fingers and then calmly picked up her teacup as if nothing had happened.

"Is . . . is that it?" Sarah said wonderingly. "Did you do it?"

"Of course. Micki's sitting home right now, hoping you'll call and ask her over to see a Godzilla movie. It starts in ten minutes."

"Wow," Sarah said, staring at the blank television screen. "You even know what's going to be on the TV."

"It's not as hard as you think." Aunt Pam laughed and held up a copy of *TV Guide*.

"Oh."

"Hurry along," Aunt Pam said. "Micki will be so glad to see you."

"I'll be glad to see her," Sarah said feelingly. "The real Micki, I mean. Not the preppy-Micki, or the jock-Micki, but the Micki who's my best friend." She started to pull on her jacket, and suddenly stopped. "Aunt Pam," she said, looking intently into her aunt's golden eyes, "everything is really back to normal, isn't it? I mean, with Micki, and the high school."

"Everything is fine, Sarah. It's just the way you want it to be, and will stay that way until — "

"Until *what*?" Sarah asked, startled.

"Well, until some new idea excites you, or some new dream strikes your fancy." She shrugged. "Then, who knows? You might find yourself casting another spell."

"No!" Sarah said, zipping up her jacket. "No more spells." She hugged her aunt. "Waterview was more than enough for me!"

As she headed down the winding wrought-iron staircase, she thought back to the midnight scene in the schoolyard. How exciting and dramatic it had been! Seeing that old Scottish castle had been a once-in-a-lifetime experience, and Sarah knew she would never forget it. If only Aunt Pam hadn't had to send it back so quickly, she thought regretfully. She would have loved to have crossed the drawbridge, and explored every single inch of it.

Then a sudden, crazy thought hit her. What if it was possible to use her powers to go back in time? What if there was a way to transport herself into a world of castles and dungeons, or maybe southern mansions and hoop skirts? All of history would be stretched out before her — all she had to do was take the plunge! It would be the riskiest thing she had ever done, and she was sure Aunt Pam would disapprove. She would say it was too reckless, and she was probably right. There would be a million questions to ask, a thousand details to work out. Yet, dangerous or not, the possibility was there. Did she dare try it?

Sarah smiled to herself, and turned up her collar against the brisk evening air as she headed home. Could she, Sarah Connell, teen witch, actually cross the time barrier?

The idea was very tempting. . . .

What do a modern teen witch and a Southern belle in the 1860's have in common? Plenty! Read Teen Witch #3, *GONE WITH THE WITCH*.